"B. Carter Pittman's stories are full of heart and hope. His tale entitled "Willie and the Twister" was particularly thrilling, utilizing intense realism coupled with tension that keeps the reader eagerly devouring every line. Another of his short pieces, "Ted," has a particularly dark note running through it that will be of interest to the historically minded. A+ for these fantastically written short-stories!"

"Debra Davis Hinkle offers a mix of both short-stories and poetry. ...I could see people identifying with some of the more painful and cathartic portions of the text. The writing had a very therapeutic quality that one might find in a personal diary or journal. The poem "Nemo" was probably my favorite."

"Shirley Radcliff Bruton's wonderful poetry has a mix of the personal and the Imagist movement within its lines. Some of my favorites include "The Blossoms and the Fence," "Impetuous Storm," and "The Old Oak Tree." Her thoughtful poems speak on themes as wide ranging as life, death, and love, but also focus on the delightfully commonplace things of everyday life, from flowers to fence rails...

"Susan Tuttle writes a mix of sci-fi and fantasy, somewhat reminiscent of 1950s writers, such as Vogt and Bradbury. ...Some stories were somewhat more contemporary in nature with differing content, particularly the samples from the Skylark series which have a more intriguing noir aspect to them."

Mark Noce, author of *Between Two Fires* and *Dark Winds Rising* (St. Martin's Press)

Tales from
a
Rocky Coast
Vol. 1

B. Carter Pittman
Debra Davis Hinkle
Shirley Radcliff Bruton
Susan Tuttle

Dac Says Publishing
San Luis Obispo, CA

Dac Says Publishing
San Luis Obispo, CA
dacsayspublishing@pacbell.net

PUBLISHING

A percentage of the profits will be donated to a charity for animals.

Special discounts are available on bulk purchases, sales promotions, fund-raising and educational needs. For details, contact the publisher at the email address above.

This is mostly a work of fiction. Names, characters, businesses, places, events and incidents are either the products of the author's imagination or used in a fictitious manner. Any resemblance to actual persons, living or dead, or actual events is purely coincidental. In the memoir, creative non-fiction and some poetry we have tried to recreate events, locales and conversations from our memories of them.

This book contains QR codes and website links. The authors do their best to control the quality of their own content. By following these QR codes and links you understand that the authors don't have control over the quality of third party content, i.e. websites and suggested videos on YouTube.

All the writers participated in the early editing process.
Project coordinator: Debra Davis Hinkle
Beta Reader: Stephanie Fusco Teaford
Book Layout: Debra Davis Hinkle using ©2018 BookDesignTemplates.com.
Copy editors: Dick Bruton, C.B. Taylor and Elaine Wolfe.
Cover design: Arron Kondziela
Starburst on cover: Donna Murphy
Authors' photo on back cover: Roland B. Hinkle
Photos embedded in Shirley Radcliff Bruton's QR codes are by Merv Lyons

Tales from a Rocky Coast, Vol. 1/ B. Carter Pittman, Debra Davis Hinkle, Shirley Radcliff Bruton and Susan Tuttle - 1st Ed. The book was printed in the United States.
ISBN-13: 978-0-9996611-0-9

Dedication

This publication takes place through the efforts of the San Luis Obispo Friday Night Writers' Group. I love these people with their heartfelt stories and vivid imaginations. The diverse writing skills, jokes and kind but firm critiques have made me a better poet and opened up new possibilities. I am very grateful.

Shirley Radcliff Bruton

A true friend is someone who is there for you when [s]he'd rather be anywhere else.

— Len Wein

This book encompasses four very different authors' work and sometimes different genres within an author's section. We have tried to edit for consistency within each section, but not necessarily from genre to genre.

More artistic license is generally accepted in poetry, so each poet is the final editor of his or her work.

Prose or poetry, sometimes we just looked to the following paragraph for editing guidance:

"When you fool around with language, freed from the constraints of conventional syntax, grammar, meaning, you can more easily access that part of the brain where creative consciousness resides." (Addonizio and Laux, The Poet's Companion, W.W. Norton & Company, 134)

Debra Davis Hinkle

TABLE OF CONTENTS

Introduction

When we think of the Friday Night Writers' Group (FNWG), a song plays in our heads:

> *Make new friends,*
> *but keep the old.*
> *One is silver*
> *and, the other gold...*

The FNWG members are solid gold. Most of us have been together between seven and fourteen years. Carter Pittman is the longest member at more than fourteen years and Debra Davis Hinkle comes in close behind him. Christine Taylor has been with the group for ten years, and Susan Tuttle arrived eight years ago. Our newest member, Shirley Radcliff Bruton, has been in the group for over a year, but she's already wormed her way into our hearts.

Each member of the group starts at a different place. One has a Master of Arts in English, another a Bachelor of Science in Business Administration (Information Systems) and still another a Bachelor of Arts in Theater, magna cum laude. A couple of members have years of computer experience—one, over thirty-five years, which is just a few years less than the age of our youngest member. Those two *nerds* dragged two others, kicking and screaming, into the 21st Century. The last one is hurrying to catch up. Some of us have been writing for most of our lives, starting somewhere in the grade school years, and others began when they joined the group. In other words, we are very diverse.

We are equally diverse in what we write: lyrical poetry, memoir, non-fiction, young adult, literary fiction, and genre fiction including sci-fi, fantasy and mystery/suspense. We produce short articles, essays, book-length non-fiction, flash fiction, short stories, novellas, novels, and everything in-between.

Our diversity makes us good at critiquing. We each have our strengths and weaknesses, and we all learn from each other. Our time together has turned silver into gold, friends, and writing-wise, too. We want the best for each other, the best being: getting published, winning awards, and ending up famous, rich, and, of course, creatively fulfilled. That last comes first, before all the rest, and is what it's all about anyway. The rest (publishing, awards, famous, and rich) is all gravy. We do love gravy, though.

We hope you enjoy reading our anthology as much as we enjoyed writing for it.

Debra Davis Hinkle
Founding member of FNWG
Facilitator of Group

Susan Tuttle
Member of FNWG

B. Carter Pittman
Founding member of the FNWG

Shirley Radcliff Bruton
Member of FNWG

SECTION ONE

B. Carter Pittman

Dedication

I dedicate my writings, first and foremost, to my wife and daughter, who continue to fill and replenish me with inspiration whenever it runs low.

I thank members of the Friday Night Writers' Group, who ensure that I dot my "I(s)" and cross my "T(s)." They are invaluable in helping me hone my skills.

I also would like to acknowledge Ms. Susan Ward, an English teacher in a small, backwater school in Colorado who saw a spark of creativity in a lonely, undirected boy and fanned it into a flame. Without her appearance and encouragement at that low point in my life, I am certain these pages would have never been written. She showed me that I had the power to create worlds, worlds that I now invite the reader to inhabit, if only for a short while.

Examples of my wife's musical ability and appreciation:

Author's Bio

B. Carter Pittman, a native of the Southwest, has lived on the Central Coast for 16 years. One of the founding members of the Friday Night Writers' group, his stories and poems have been included in various publications over the past 20 years. His genres are as eclectic as his subjects, ranging from memoir to science fiction/fantasy, some of which have won writing awards.

"Like my characters, I like to explore," says Pittman, "and what better way than from behind a keyboard, where the possibilities are infinite?"   Pittman lives with his wife Ravelle, daughter Lyla, as well as Noche, an enormous black dog, and Binx, a small—but extremely suave—black cat.

TED

One could put the drunks at our local inn into four distinct groups. First, there were the friendly, affable drunks who cracked jokes and bought everyone rounds. Normally, these were most commonly seen every payday, but progressively less until the next payday. Then came the lovable slobs, who delighted in throwing an arm over your shoulders and foul breath in your face as they swore undying friendship and fealty to you, whether they knew you or not. This showering of affection would last until one either elbowed them in the ribs or bought them a drink, the latter being what they were after in the first place.

The third group consisted of the straight arrow, tell-it-like-it-is tosspots who would, for no apparent reason, be compelled to stare you in the eye and declare, in slushy voices, that they'd never told a lie. They might steal your drink or the change you left on the bar, but they'd always own up to it if you caught them.

Last, and in my mind least, came the tough, bruiser-boozers who felt they weren't getting their due respect, and to whom lingering eye contact was an affront and a challenge. Buoyed by the fear and dread they instilled in their wives and children, they felt it extended to everyone else. They were often taught otherwise, but would return after their contusions had faded, talking smack once again.

All four groups were amusing to watch for about an hour, after which they would merge into one sloppy, homogenous group of imbeciles. It was soon after the four groups had merged on one cold, January night when my two older sisters and I met Ted.

Our parents had decided to have dinner and a night out and, rather than leave us to our own devices at home, took us with them. After dinner, when the dancing started and the liquor began flowing more freely, we were sequestered to the front of the establishment with the pool-and-foosball tables, as well as an ancient pinball machine. Having played them all multiple times, we tired of them (I ran out of quarters) and were soon bored out of our wits. We were ready to go home, but our folks loved to dance, so we knew we were in it for the long haul.

The front door of the inn opened to admit a tall man who proceeded to dust snowflakes from his hair and sweater. He stomped clumps of snow from his boots onto the rubber mat, and then walked up to the bar and ordered a drink.

The newcomer nursed his drink in silence at a corner table while his gaze flicked all over the room, seeming to itemize everything it touched. He wasn't a local, so I thought he was probably either coming from, or going to, one of the many nearby ski resorts. The San Luis Valley in Colorado began to get tourists year-round.

I also noticed that even the most brazen of the drunks avoided conversing with him, though he did nothing, overtly, to dissuade them.

"Think Mom and Dad'll keep it up 'til closing time again?" Debbie mumbled, gloomy stare fixed on the cracked, vinyl booth-back across from her. She had the look of one who already knew the terrible truth, but felt compelled to ask anyway.

"Whaddaya think?" came Dianne's acerbic reply as she twirled her blonde locks in endless circles. With the sigh of a deflating tire, Debbie closed her eyes and propped her chin in her hands, letting her long, brown hair fall over her face to shut out the world.

"Got any change, Dianne?"

"No, Carter, just like I didn't when you asked two minutes ago! Go bug Mom and Dad for some."

"I already tried," I said, crestfallen. "They won't stop dancing long enough for me to ask."

"Then shut up about it."

"Yeah, quit whining," Debbie seconded from beneath her shroud of hair, "and move over. I don't want your fleas hopping onto me."

"Don't worry, your lice would crowd them out!" popped my snappy comeback. The three of us scowled at one another (Debbie from behind her hair) for a long moment before lapsing once more into a morose silence. I found a skull-shaped spot on the wall to study.

"You guys look so excited that you can barely contain yourselves!"

We looked up to see the stranger leaning against our booth. He chuckled when Debbie emerged from her hair, snorted, and rolled her eyes in response. He glanced at me, then gestured out into the center of the room.

"Why aren't you out there burning up that pool table, Sport?"

"It takes money, which I ain't got," came my sullen reply.

He grinned and stuck out a well-manicured hand. "I'm Ted. What's your name?"

I shook it. "Carter."

"Here, Carter." He reached into his pocket and pulled out a fist laden with coins, "take this and go play some pool—it's on me."

Ted proffered the largest handful of change I'd ever seen and, in the '70s, quite a boon for an 11-year-old boy.

The temptation was strong, but my folks' teachings were stronger: *never accept anything from strangers.*

"No thanks," I said as my darker half simultaneously railed at the unfairness of it all: *It wasn't as if I asked him for the money,* whined the ongoing litany, *all he wants is for me to disappear so he can talk to these stupid girls.*

An eager "I'll take 'em!" announced the sudden appearance of my friend Kyle, who didn't share my compunctions against taking gifts from strangers.

Holding my eyes, the man slowly poured the change into Kyle's cupped hands with dramatic effect, saying, "Now *here's* a boy who knows a great opportunity when it comes along!" Shifting his attention to Kyle, he jerked his head toward me and said, "Bet you could show him a thing or two at the pool table too, huh?"

"Aw, I smoke Carter all the time!"

Well, that was true enough. Kyle's folks ran the inn, so he had much more time to practice than I. Still, his comment rankled and carried an unspoken challenge. I went to the rack and selected a cue as Kyle gleefully slid a couple of quarters into the table's change slots. As the balls thundered down the chute, I thought I saw a triumphant smirk on Ted's face before he turned his full attention to my sisters. Something about him didn't seem right. I couldn't put my finger on it.

"Hey!"

"What?"

"You deaf?" Kyle sneered. "The game's Last Pocket. You rack."

As our game progressed, I watched Kyle's and my benefactor as he talked to Dianne and Debbie. Too far away to hear everything, I heard parts of the conversation. He talked animatedly about his VW Bug.

Why is he wasting his time talking to them? I wondered. Though young, he was clearly too old for a couple of teenage girls—fifteen and seventeen. True, it was slim pickings at that particular inn, but still—to my way of thinking, at least—a person would have to be pretty damn desperate to single out *my* sisters.

"Hellooo?"

Kyle jarred me back to the task at hand. "Huh?"

Rolling his eyes, Kyle enunciated each word. "Eight. Ball. In. The. Side. Pocket."

I hadn't been paying much attention to the game; the odd drama going on at the booth seemed more interesting. Not surprisingly, most of my balls were still on the table as Kyle lined up his final shot with care, and then sent the cue ball rocketing toward the eight. The eight ball obligingly rolled into the pocket as planned but, to Kyle's misfortune, was then followed by the white. Kyle had "scratched" and lost the game.

"Sonofamuthafuckinbitch!"

"Haaa!" I shouted in false triumph, then came a shrill roar:

"*Kyle!* Get your filthy, foul-mouthed butt over here! *Now!*"

"Oh, shit!" squeaked Kyle, the personification of hopelessness and fear.

Kyle's misfortune had a cascading effect; his mother had overheard the last exclamation as well. Wearing the expression of a damned soul, Kyle shuffled over to where his angry mother waited. Grabbing him by the scruff of the neck, she propelled him through the bat-winged doors leading into the kitchen, and to whatever grisly fate awaited him.

Poor bastard, I wisely thought to myself, rather than voiced. Kyle would be elbow-deep in dishwater for the remainder of the night, probably sporting a sore ass. With pool opponent and money gone in one fell swoop, I meandered back over to where Ted and the girls were talking.

"... all at once, of course, because the back seat's full of my stuff, but there's room for one passenger at a time. It's parked right outside the door, and I wouldn't mind taking you each for a short spin around the block. No problem at all."

Dianne, the oldest and most diplomatic of the two girls, said, "I've always thought it would be fun to ride in a VW Bug, but it's too cold outside to enjoy it. Besides, our folks wouldn't like it."

Ted affected a devil-may-care look and said, *sotto voce*, "What they don't know won't hurt you!"

"They're just in the next room," Debbie piped up.

"Yeah... but they're so busy dancing, they won't know you're gone before you're back again. You'd be gone for two, three minutes tops. C'mon, live dangerously for once— unless, of course, you find staring at peeling wallpaper more a-*peeling*." He chuckled at his own wit.

I popped up like a gadfly. "Why?"

Ted's toothy smile didn't reach his eyes as he regarded me. "Because VW Bugs are fun to drive, and these two have never experienced one."

"I've never ridden in one, either," I volunteered. Just to twist the knife, I added, "Can I go, too?"

"Well," he smiled good-naturedly as his eyes screamed *miserable little cock-block*! "as I was just explaining, there isn't enough room for all of us to go at once, but I can sure take you for a spin just as soon as they've had their turns, little buddy!"

Dianne, catching onto my little game, made an unsuccessful attempt to hide her grin. Debbie looked contemplatively into her soda glass, shook the ice around a little, and then sucked the last couple of slurps out of it with her straw.

Making a valiant effort to hide his fury, Ted beamed at me for a couple of ticks before turning back to the girls. "So, how about it?"

"Well, you seem like a nice man, and it's sure good of you to offer, Ted," said Dianne the diplomat, "but we really can't. Our folks are going to want to go home any minute now. Besides," she added, looking him straight in the eyes, "you wouldn't want us to get in the habit of going off with someone we just met, now would you? Wouldn't that be a little dangerous?"

Ted's demeanor changed in an instant.

"Suit yourselves," he said, brusque and cold. "Too bad, though—you struck me as a couple of free-spirited gals. Guess I was wrong."

That said, he downed his drink and walked out into the night without another word. A gust of wind blew in swirling flakes of snow as the door closed behind him, chilling us.

"What a *weirdo*!" Debbie snorted. "Who gives a shit about riding around in a VW?"

"I don't think that was all he wanted," came Dianne's sage reply.

"Yeah, I caught that. I'm not an idiot, you know."

My folks walked up before my sisters could get into a heated discussion about each other's I.Q., and we all finally went home.

It wasn't the last we heard of Ted, though. A few nights later, on a newscast, we learned that his last name was Bundy.

For more information, scan the QR code to Biography.com

WILLIE AND THE TWISTER

Back in '69, my family lived in an old, rambling farmhouse about a mile outside of Olton, Texas. My memories of that time period are idyllic: playing in the forest of corn stalks surrounding our house, the sweet (and often sour) notes heard during my sisters' piano lessons, homemade ice cream, and catching horned toads. It was a time when life's paint still seemed fresh, and the world a more mysterious, wondrous place for me, when my only major problem came in the form of a Rhode Island Red rooster I had dubbed "Willie."

Being small for my age, Willie, a large, fierce bird, had me fairly cowed. Whenever he spotted me crossing the barnyard, he'd come pelting after me, head down and feathers ruffled. I would often run rather than stand my ground, at which times my sisters, Dianne and Debbie, would laugh out loud and call me the "chicken of chickens." Other than a few scratches and pecks, Willie never really hurt me, though my pride took a beating.

I thought myself pretty brave about most things; did I not punch Wayne DuPreast in the belly when he called me "Shorty"?—with him a whole head taller than me! Willie, though... I couldn't reason with, nor intimidate him; he was an animal, pure and simple, and he kept coming at me, no matter what I did. That made him a formidable opponent in my eyes.

My father once advised: "He's like every other bully; if you'll face that rooster down instead of run, he'll leave you alone."

As a testament to my trust in Dad, I stood my ground... right up to the moment Willie flew in my face and made me trip and fall down, at which point he jumped on my back and furiously pecked my head until I regained my feet and took off. To this day, I can clearly see Dad shaking his head, an expression of disappointment stamped on his features as I ran past with Willie in hot pursuit. Perhaps he never forgot the look of betrayal on mine, either. I began carrying a long stick with me whenever I went into the barnyard, and with it I held Willie at bay most of the time, but every once in a while he would slip through my defenses and put me to flight. It became a war of attrition between us. Other than having my own personal harpy, though, life seemed blissful and ordinary for me.

Early one June afternoon, I found my mother and father standing on the back porch, looking at the bank of thunderheads rolling majestically in from the Southwest. The clouds wouldn't reach us for another hour or two, but I could already smell rain on the cool breeze that preceded them.

"That looks like a tornado rack, Bill." Mom's brows were knitted in worry as she looked up in his face. A gusting breeze tugged at the ties and tail of her gauze headscarf.

My father nodded. "It is. Look over yonder." He pointed at a section of the still-distant cloud bank where what looked like a puppy's tail dropped from beneath the bank, squiggled a bit, and then receded back into the clouds.

"A funnel," Dad explained. "None of them have touched ground yet, but we'd better listen to the weather reports from here on out, and get ready to go to the cellar." He took another sip of his coffee, peering over the rim of his cup at the approaching storm.

"Guess I'd better get supper cooked before the stove's blown away," quipped my mother as she went back into the house.

I remained on the porch with Dad, watching the dazzling display of far-off lightning. Worry shadowed his bronzed, weathered features as he scanned the darkening sky from horizon to horizon. After a while, he glanced down at me doing my best impersonation of him. He grinned and reached down to muss my always-ruffled hair.

"Well, guess I'd better round up some candles and blankets for the storm cellar—looks like we might be needing 'em. You'd better come in too." I looked in the direction he nodded his head, "I noticed that rooster's been edging closer and closer since we've stood here."

"I ain't 'fraid a' him!"

Dad shrugged, throwing the remainder of his coffee on the ground. "Suit yourself," his mouth quirking up on one side as he turned away.

He's laughing at me! The realization stung. *I'll show him!*

I stayed rooted to the spot. As he'd said, Willie inched ever closer, scratching and pecking the ground as if looking for delectable bugs and other tidbits, but keeping one beady eye locked on me all the while. When he came close enough by his estimation, he dropped the charade and charged, feathers unfurled.

In a pathetic show of defiance, I stepped behind the safety of the screen door with as much nonchalance as expedience would allow. Willlie danced his usual small victory circle—with one wing dipped and dragging on the opposite side of the screen.

In a sudden burst of spite, I shoved the door open and knocked him squawking off the porch, shouting, "Get back, you stupid *hen*!"

Surprised, Willie left off his little dance, made an offended "Puh-PUH-puh-puh-puh!" noise, and then high-stepped it back to the chicken house.

I felt a little better about myself for my cruelty.

I found Dad in the storage room, taking a dusty kerosene lamp down from the top shelf and setting it beside a collection of candles, a jug of water, a transistor radio, spare batteries, and old blankets.

"Here, Carter—grab those candles for me, will you? Can you carry the radio too? Good! We might be able to take it all down in one shot."

"Dianne says there're Black Widders in the cellar, Dad."

"Your sisters say a lot of things to scare you, and you just make it too easy for them." He sighed, then added, "I put some bug poison down there a few days ago... you'll be all right."

I lapsed into a sullen silence, frustrated by how everything I said and did at the time called to question my courage.

When Dad and I tramped outside with our burdens, the wind had picked up, and the sky had grown much darker as clouds obscured the sun. I could hear an almost constant roll of thunder, muffled by the distance. Willie appeared to have retired to the chicken house for the day. In the corral, the calves were frisking around, energized by the approaching storm. Little Bit, our dog, already cowered from the thunder. He watched our goings-on from the sanctuary of his mat in the well house, once in a while giving voice to his despair with a mournful howl.

"Oh, it's just terrible, isn't it?" Dad called to the dog. "Silly ol' mutt," he murmured, chuckling as he pulled open the heavy cellar door.

"Are we gonna bring Little Bit down with us if we hafta go to the cellar?"

"Not unless you want to get nipped, like the last time you tried to drag him in there. I think he'd rather take his chances where he is." Dad then clicked on the flashlight and descended into the cellar's inky, musty depths, where a multitude of insects scuttled for cover from the sudden light.

So much for the bug poison, I thought. I figured Little Bit had a point.

Dad set his bundle down on an old, dusty table, and then relieved me of mine as well. He surveyed our surroundings with a critical eye. Fruit jars with nameless contents sat exactly where previous tenants had placed them on shelves, years ago. Gnarled roots and tubers hung from the roof beams on wires. A rusty sprocket lay on the floor next to a dented, metal bucket. A coil of rope hung on a nail driven in one of the support posts.

"Run and get the broom and dustpan for me, would you?"

I fetched the two items for him, but I ended up on the business end of them. Still, the cellar was small, and I was more than happy to sweep spiders, centipedes, and scorpions from their havens to end up squished beneath our shoes.

"Don't step on the stink bugs," Dad instructed. Those we gingerly swept up whole into the pan, and dumped them outside with their squashed compatriots.

Several minutes of furious sweeping and stomping later, Dad squeezed my shoulder and said, "That's most of them." Winking, he added, "Save a couple of bugs to crawl up your sisters' legs." I laughed long and hard, picturing what would happen. Grinning, he stooped and picked up the dustpan. "Let's go wash up and eat."

A gale-force wind greeted us when we emerged from the cellar, and a few fat drops of rain accompanied it.

"D'ya think we'll be staying in the cellar tonight, Dad?"

"Maybe. We'll listen to the weather reports."

When we got inside, Mom had the table set. "There you are," she sighed. "Thank God I didn't have to go out in that to get you."

"What's the weather report, Hon?"

"There's a tornado watch, but no alerts so far. Hopefully, this will blow over without dropping a twister."

Dad looked dubious. "Lord willing, but there were plenty of bubbles in that rack, last time I looked. If not," Dad clapped me on the shoulder, "well, that cellar needed a good cleaning, anyway."

Supper consisted of chicken-fried steak, spinach, mashed potatoes, gravy, and a salad. After Dad's ritual mealtime prayer, the five of us fell-to with gusto, all but ignoring the wind howling outside and the occasional, tooth-rattling boom of thunder. Rain drummed our roof in such a constant barrage that it sounded like a waterfall pouring on the house. The crackling radio sat on the nearby kitchen counter, pulling sentry duty against possible tornadoes by keeping us posted with the latest reports.

We were just into our meal when Dad suddenly held up his hand, shushing us all into motionless silence as he listened intently to the tinny voice on the radio:

"... repeat, this is a tornado alert for the areas of Earth, Dimmit, and Olton, Texas, and surrounding communities. Listeners are advised to immediately go to the nearest emergency shelters and remain there until further notice."

Dad wiped his mouth with a napkin, pushed back from the table and said, around a mouthful of food, "Let's go."

With Dad leading the way and Mom hustling us kids in front of her, we grabbed our raincoats from their hooks in the hallway as we filed past. The sudden blast of wind and rain as I stepped out of the door would have knocked me off of my feet had Mom not had a firm grip on my arm. Bending into the gale, we traversed the distance to the cellar and descended the steps. Fighting the wind, Dad struggled to shut and latch the heavy door behind us as Mom lit some candles. Shadows danced on the cellar walls in the flickering light. My sisters and I took the opportunity to make shadow creatures with our hands. I managed to make a fairly decent rabbit, but Debbie could make a horse's head, and Dianne could do several animals.

"Look out, Carter," Dianne taunted, "I made a chicken! Run!"

I shoved her hard in the back, causing her to lurch forward and knock over a candle.

"You kids better settle down right now," Mom shrilled. "A tornado's nothing compared to what I can do to you!"

Having secured the door to his satisfaction, Dad skuffed down the steps to join us, breathing hard from his exertions and soaked to the skin. "Bonnie, why are you lighting those candles? Why didn't you light the coal-oil lamp?"

"Because that damned thing is dangerous and it makes me nervous to mess with it," She cocked an eyebrow at him. "*You* light it."

Dad obligingly struck a match, lifted the globe a bit, and lit the wick. It cast a dim flicker until he raised the wick by turning a small wheel, after which the cellar flooded with light. The lamp smelled strongly and had a menacing hiss, but the added light made the cellar less dismal, plus it helped keep the remaining creepy-crawlies at bay. Mom blew out the candles; pungent smoke writhed up from the extinguished wicks.

How can mere words describe how it felt in that cellar, that feeling of safety derived from being in a hole in the ground, all the while knowing that everything above our heads could be getting destroyed at that very moment? I can clearly recall everything about our small, humble sanctuary, as if it weren't a lifetime ago. My mind's eye yet follows lurid shadows dancing on the walls; the smells of must, candle wax, and kerosene assail my nostrils with the slightest conjuring of memory. The most vivid impression of all, however, is the constant, terrible roar of the storm; its echoes continue to rage after four decades.

Were we there for an hour? Four hours? I couldn't really say—time becomes meaningless in a confined space, where minutes are like hours, and an hour is an eternity. It seems as if a small piece of my soul remained, abandoned in time to haunt that cellar, occasionally sending impressions to the present.

"An all-clear has been given for the areas surrounding Earth, Dimmit, and Olton, Texas. Once again, the National Weather Service has issued an all-clear for the areas... " the announcer droned on amidst the static.

Elated, it didn't take us long to grab our few items and emerge from our stygian cell.

The bulk of the storm seemed to have passed, leaving behind large mud puddles, which we skirted with care after a sharp word from Mom. Little Bit greeted us, tail a wagging blur. The house and outbuildings proved to still be standing under dad's flashlight beam.

"Well, if there actually was a twister, it must've missed us," said Dad.

We slogged through the mire to the house, shedding our muddy shoes at the door at Mom's insistence. We returned to our interrupted supper, cold but edible, and continued the meal. Afterwards, we all retired to the den to watch an episode of *Mission: Impossible*.

I can't remember which one of us noticed it first, but we heard what sounded like a continuous blast of the horn of a truck or freight train, growing louder. Dad lunged out of his chair and bolted into the adjacent laundry room to look out of the window.

"Bonnie, come here!" There was a quality to his voice I had never heard before, and it caused my insides to turn to ice when I recognized it: fear.

Mom hurried to the laundry room, us kids in tow. I looked out the window to see an impossibly immense and undulating pillar, stretching up into infinity. The twister appeared mostly black, but glowed red down the center, and each side looked like a sheet of blue ice. Like the finger of a malevolent god, it sketched a line through the corn stalks straight towards us, promising certain death with its touch. **Doom** had arrived, with the voice of a thousand jet engines.

It was far too late to run for the cellar, situated between the tornado and us. Had we attempted to seek its shelter, we would most likely have been swept up into the twister's maw. I couldn't hear Mom's scream over the cacophony of the tornado, but I could see it on her face, and feel it in her vice-like grip as she hauled the three of us into the long entrance hallway where we sat on the floor, huddled like fugitives.

Meanwhile, Dad ran throughout the house slamming open several windows. Although his actions were mystifying at the time, I later understood that he attempted to equalize the pressure inside the house with the outside, so that it wouldn't be blown apart like matchsticks. He soon joined the rest of us in the hall, adding his death grip to my mother's.

All we could do at that point was wait for nature's verdict. My thoughts were many in those frantic moments, but among them came the irrational, irreverent wish: *I hope it gets ol' Willie!* I didn't even have the decency to feel ashamed of myself.

The telephone rang.

Mom shouted, "Don't answer it, Bill!"

Longtime residents of tornado country, my folks knew that, during a storm, static electricity could build-up in the lines—or possibly a fallen power line may cross with a telephone wire—putting a lethal charge of voltage into telephones, causing them to ring.

Dad shot Mom a hacked look.

"Do you honestly think I would get up and answer the damned phone at a time like this?"

Had I not been so terrified, I would have laughed at the conversation.

We could hear nails protesting from the massive den roof being pulled from the walls. The noise had reached its crescendo when we heard—and felt—a tremendous slam that shook the entire house.

We trembled in our family knot for a long time before we noticed that the noise had abated. We all wore the same look of wonder as we slowly eased our grips on one another. Dad got up to investigate, but when we kids tried to follow, Mom pulled us back down to the floor. After a while, Dad came back and announced that the tornado had passed; the slamming we had heard had been the den roof settling back into place after the tornado had released it from its grip. Crying, Mom rocked us in her arms and said a prayer of thanks before releasing us.

We all went outside and looked up into a clear, starry sky; the storm had moved past us. A short while later, spotlights shone on our house from the highway as emergency workers searched for damaged homes. Dad waved his arms to indicate that we were okay, and they moved on to see if others needed help.

We piled into the car and went to check on our neighbors. Our nearest ones, less than a quarter-mile away from us, had been watching television when their living room roof had been pulled off over their heads. Their large farm truck had been twisted in such a way that the front tires were resting on the ground, but the back tires were sticking up to the sky. The massive elm tree in their front yard had been snapped in half. I noticed a flimsy piece of board impossibly going in one side of the stump and out the other. Miraculously, the couple had been unharmed. A few days later, my sisters and I would find their roof in a stock tank about half a mile away from their house.

We were relieved to learn that, aside from some minor damage here and there, our other neighbors had weathered the storm in one piece. When we returned home, Little Bit emerged from the well house to greet us, his tail tucked, but wagging all the same.

We soon discovered that huge swaths of corn stalks had been uprooted and scattered in a rough, two-acre circle around our home. The tornado had jumped and landed on top of us, putting our house and outbuildings directly within its eye before it jumped again. Death had circled us, tugged on us, then left us unscathed. We didn't doubt the power of prayer after that night.

Things quickly returned to normal. The next morning, as if privy to the dark thought that had raced through my mind the previous night, an angry, very much alive Willie waited for me. With little preamble he, all feathers and fury, made his usual, obligatory attack. Things were different that morning, though; I did not run, nor did I brandish my stick. After he hit my leg full-force, I simply nudged him aside and kept on walking.

THE GEMINI PORTAL

This is an excerpt from a work in progress.

Chapter I

A glimpse over the rainbow

"Well shit, Jigger, this is...What the hell is it?"

Some of the greatest discoveries have come about by accident, when the inventor is attempting to do something else. Logan Black felt that his experiment stood in mute testimony of that fact. Transfixed and barely breathing, his attention remained riveted on the image before him.

"Woof!"

Despite the gravity of the moment, Logan grinned and turned to his companion—a huge, black dog sitting on an extra-large cushion on the floor. Jigger thumped his tail when his master looked at him.

"I know, right?   Exciting! But what the hell is it?"

This last sentence trailed off in an awed whisper as Logan took a deep, fortifying breath and lowered his arms from their warding positions. He wrestled his initial panic down to the pit of his stomach where it fluttered, threatening to flare up once again. Logan turned his attention once more to the object that appeared moments ago.

The scene before him seemed rather ordinary: a down-sloping, grassy field interspersed with stunted shrubs. A tumultuous sea lay beyond which, in turn, extended to the horizon. The view one could find on a multitude of coasts around the world: picturesque, yes, but not uncommon.

This particular view however, defied rational physics, even sanity—because it was impossible.

The fact that the landscape was contained in an upright oval limned by a neon-blue nimbus, hovering about six inches above the concrete floor of the 40 x 25-foot Quonset-hut-cum-workshop *made* it impossible.

The oval had a width of close to four feet at its widest, and a height of perhaps six. The electrical cord to the Plexiglas box and speakers, which used to fill that space, still dangled from the bottom of the nimbus, suspended in midair.

Closer inspection showed that the land features remained unchanged as he walked a complete circle around the anomaly. It always presented the same view, regardless of where he positioned himself.

He also discovered that, although the oval remained stationary, land features contained in its foreground noticeably receded as he moved away from it, and enlarged when he drew near, as with objects under normal circumstances.

From his vantage point, looking straight into the portal (as he had begun to think of it), Logan could see miles of open space but, if he walked around the image, he would see that his workshop wall remained in place.

There was no "back" or "side" to the anomaly; 3-dimensional and confined to a finite space, it resembled a holographic projection...sans projector. The image looked too real to be a projected image.

If it is *real*, he thought, *what keeps* that *place out of this one—or* this *place out of that one? Is this like a...Black Hole? If it is, this could...!*

A thread of panic unwound from the pit of his stomach and lashed around his vocal cords:

"*Ohfuckmeeee*, Jigger!" he hissed, "What the hell have I done?"

In response, Jigger cocked his head one way, then the other.

"Shit!" Logan exclaimed, louder, but the added volume elicited no solution. He didn't often resort to foul language, but it seemed legit under the current circumstances. "Shitohshitohshit!"

He looked at the electrical cord dangling beneath. He almost lunged to yank it out of the socket, but stayed his hand. He couldn't bring himself to wipe out of existence what could be the greatest discovery in centuries, accidental or not.

Logan once more opted for calm, taking steady, deep breaths. He further soothed himself by realizing that he hadn't, as of yet anyway, been sucked into the alien landscape.

Logan Black frowned in concentration as he examined the contents of the oval.

There. *Movement*! He noted that the grass in the image writhed, as if its blades were animate and struggling to wriggle out of the soil. Leaves in the small shrubs acted much the same way, as if agitated by a stiff breeze, yet their branches didn't bend as one might expect in conjunction with the movement of the leaves.

Perplexed but calmer, Logan decided to conduct a few simple experiments to determine the properties of the anomaly. He ripped out a sheet of paper from a legal pad and wadded it up. Hearing commotion behind him, Logan looked back to see Jigger had surged to his feet at the sight of the paper ball.

"No. Stay, Jigger. Lay down."

Jigger offered a hacked, go-to-hell look that only a dog could deliver and then, with a disgruntled groan, flopped down.

"Good boy. Stay there." Logan turned his attention back to the task at hand.

Will this go through the image and land on the other side of the room, or will it land in the image? Logan tossed it, and grunted in amazement when the paper ball landed on the grass—*in the image*. He quickly walked to the other side of the oval and confirmed that the paper wasn't there.

It's not just an image, then.

"It's some kind of—some kind of doorway—a portal, Jigger!" he announced.

Jigger merely cocked an ear.

"Aw, c'mon you mutt—even *you* can't be blasé about this!"

Jigger rose one brow, then the other before huffing out another sigh with a token thump of his tail, as if to say *Yeah, yeah—it's amazing. Now let me go to sleep.*

"Oh yeah, sure—you see this shit all the time, don't you?" Logan looked back at the oval.

The paper ball was gone.

Logan quickly tore off a second sheet from the legal pad and repeated the process. This time his attention remained riveted to the paper. The wad of paper remained in the same spot, though it seemed to vibrate in place. Suddenly it moved, rolling out of view within seconds.

"Holy...this is some crazy shit!" Logan whooped, clapped his hands together and barked a hysteria-tinged laugh.

Choosing Jigger as his anchor to reality, Logan walked over to where he lay and idly scratched behind the dog's ears as he considered the situation.

"Does this...thing...present a danger, Jigger? And, if so, what kind of danger? Are the paper balls somewhere nearby? Across the planet? Across the universe or in *another* universe?

"Are they over the rainbow, Auntie Em?" Logan sat in silence for a long moment, staring in wonder at the anomaly. "Cause that sure doesn't look like Kansas to *me*, Jigger. It surely doesn't."

* * *

As a list of potential hazards marched across his mind, Logan felt a resurgence of his initial panic. Again, he forced it down and reminded himself that the object had remained unchanged. Whatever, *wherever* it was, it seemed stable and contained in the nimbus.

"Okay, Jigger—we know objects can go *into* the thing, but can they come out?"

Jigger remained motionless, eyes closed.

"Right. Look, I'm sorry I couldn't let you chase the paper ball. Later, okay?"

Crickets.

Giving up trying to cheer the disconsolate dog, Logan cast his gaze around the room, looking for something else to throw in the portal, something heavier than a paper ball.

His attention fell upon a small, ball-peen hammer. He snatched it up, hefted it, and then carried it to a cabinet where he pulled out a length of nylon cord. Fastening one end of the rope under the head of the hammer, he took the contrivance close to the portal.

"You ready for this, Jigger? One small throw for Man...!"

Hearing the excitement in his master's voice, Jigger opened one eye and spared Logan with a brief, monocular glance.

"You are *such* a buzz-kill, Jigger."

Logan swung his arm back and forth a few times, then let fly the hammer toward the portal, holding tightly to the end of the rope. The hammer landed soundlessly in the grass.

Logan watched it for several seconds. The hammer remained in place amongst the writhing blades of grass, but the thin cord vibrated, as if alive. Logan took a deep breath, and then tugged on it. The hammer moved toward him rapidly, at a rate seemingly faster than Logan had pulled.

As his hands grasped the portion of the rope that had been in the portal, he noticed that it felt subtly warmer. When the hammer came through, he had to jump to one side to avoid being struck by it.

"Damn!" Logan exclaimed as the hammer rebounded with a clang off the concrete floor behind him. He shot a glance at the portal, expecting to see someone—or some*thing*—there that might have thrown it in the last seconds. Nothing.

Shaken, he made his way to a nearby work stool and plopped on it, never taking his gaze off the anomaly.

"Damn..." he breathed. "I've gotta sort this thing out." He ran his fingers through his hair.

Logan grabbed the legal pad, flipped to a clean page and began jotting down information—time, date, and the order of events. Every time he started to write something down, his gaze was drawn inexorably back to the portal.

"Let's go to the house, Jigger," Logan said with a sigh. "I can't focus with this thing in the same room... not right now, anyway."

Jigger lumbered to his feet and stretched with a groan, then padded to the door. Logan backed out after him, unwilling to turn his back on the anomaly.   After closing the door, he put the padlock in the latch and snapped it shut. He wasn't ready for this, and he sure as *hell* wasn't ready to explain it to anyone wandering into the workshop.

Chapter II

A Burden Shared

Logan followed Jigger up the gently sloping path to the house. He and Ellen had bought the old farmhouse, a fixer-upper, about five years ago. He paused in the path for a few moments, looking at it. It evoked bittersweet feelings every time he allowed himself to ruminate about it.

We had such plans. Baby, if I could just...

He forced his thoughts away from the what-might-have-beens—those dangerous waters that threatened to overflow his lids and flood his cheeks. Ellen was gone. The baby was gone. Forever. He began striding up the path once more, forcing his thoughts to return to the enigma in his shop.

Should I cut the power to the Quonset? What would happen then? Would I be able to get it back? A diligent note keeper, he could duplicate everything he had done up to the moment it appeared, but would he want to? Might it be unstable next time?

Jigger waited for him beside his bowls, an expectant look on his face. His tail thumped against the kitchen cabinet.

"What? You expecting something?"

Jigger continued to thump, staring up at him.

"Oh, all right. Not that you deserve it, the way you acted in the shop." Logan scooped dog food out of the bin and dumped it into Jigger's bowl. Logan dumped his water and replenished it with fresh.

"If that's all, I'll see to myself now, Your Highness."

Jigger remained focused on the remaining handful of kibbles left in his bowl.

"Sarcasm's lost on you, isn't it?"

Logan opened the refrigerator and looked inside. The scene was grim: a nigh-empty carton of milk, a half-eaten packet of bologna well past its expiration date, half an onion, and a package of hamburger meat he took out of the freezer two days ago. A few beers lay scattered on the shelves. He poked the package of meat and grunted when it gave a little. Thawed.

Setting the meat on the counter, he went to the walk-in pantry and searched the shelves, finally selecting a can of mixed vegetables.

Twenty minutes later saw him eating a fried hamburger patty with a mixture of corn, green beans, and carrots. His simple fare brought his wife to mind yet again, as did many little things. He chuckled, thinking of what she might have said had he placed this meal in front of her. Jigger would have had *two* meals in a row.

Logan was pulled from his thoughts when he heard a familiar rumble coming up his long drive. Only one person he knew made such a racket: Toby, in his ancient Chevy truck.

"Looks like we've got company, Jigger," he called out— then heard the sound of the pet door open and close; Jigger was already on it. The lack of booming barks further indicated that it was Toby. Toby was Jigger's second— possibly first— favorite person in the whole world.

The screen door creaked open and banged shut. Heavy footsteps tromped into the kitchen, paused near the stove, and then continued on into the dining room. Toby's tall, lanky frame soon filled the doorway.

"Really, don't bother to knock," Logan muttered around a mouthful of hamburger.

"Oh, I won't," came the baritone reply.   Toby grinned at his friend.   "I think it's rude to bang on someone else's house. Don't you?"

Logan chuckled. "Had anything to eat, yet?"

"Nah, but I'm not too hungry," Toby replied, eyeing Logan's plate, "not *that* hungry, anyway."

"Ungrateful bastard," Logan muttered without heat.

Toby grinned and shrugged. "Sorry, but a fried, lukewarm hamburger patty swimming in grease and canned veggies are right up there with...say...road kill."

"Then by all means, why don't you go grab some of that? There's a skunk about three days fresh a mile down the road.   Can't miss it."

"Actually, I didn't—why do you think it's there?" Toby slapped a drum roll on the dining room table.

Both men laughed at their ridiculous repartee.   Toby had a way of breaking him out of his shell. He didn't tiptoe around Logan like the rest of his friends had after Ellen died, as though one wrong word might send him into an emotional abyss. Logan was miserable, not fragile.   Toby got it.

Logan cocked an eyebrow at his friend, narrowly regarding him.

Should I tell him about the experiment? he thought. *I need to tell someone I trust.*

"Well, Tobias—what brings you to the boonies? Aside from insulting my cuisine, that is."

Toby pulled back a chair, spun it around, and plopped down, forearms dangling over the backrest.   Logan thought his long, narrow face was seven notches below handsome and five above butt-ugly.   The numbers changed, depending on grooming. Ellen had once described him as "ruggedly handsome," but Logan thought she was being kind. Lank, dark brown hair lay plastered against

Toby's gently sloping forehead, indicating he'd recently done some strenuous, sweaty work.

"Ah, nothing to write home about. Just finished a job for ol' Connie Fryeburg down the road. Crawled under her house for half a day—dodging black widows and fixing her pipes. Glad that nightmare's over."

"You kidding?" Logan snorted. "It's never over with her! Mark my words, she'll be bugging you about something else broken—and she'll say it was *your* fault."

"You're probably right. At least it's over for the moment, anyway." Toby reached over and picked up the saltshaker, then began rolling it back and forth between his palms.

"Hard job, huh?" Logan asked, stabbing the last morsel of hamburger patty with his fork.

"Oh, the work I didn't mind—it's *her* I can't stand!" Toby began lightly tapping the end of the shaker against the table.

He's agitated, Logan observed.

"She stiffed me for an hour's work, said that she wouldn't pay for the time that I *wasted* going for parts."

"Figures." Logan shook his head. "She's a real piece of work, that one. Lived off a fat trust fund all her life, yet thinks she knows more about what is, and isn't, considered work than anyone else. Even Ellen couldn't stand her."

"That Ellen was a fine judge of character, though she *did* marry you. Guess you can't be right on the mark every time." Toby grinned, showing long, white teeth in stark contrast to his bronzed skin.

"I quite agree," Logan replied. "Want a beer?"

"What do you think I'm here for—the scintillating conversation and cuisine?"

"Then let's get to it, and raise a toast to haggish trust-funders everywhere."

Logan was surprised at how easily his friend pulled his thoughts away from the portal in his shop.

Earth-shattering and normal... may the twain never meet, he pled to the universe.

Logan carried his plate and fork to the sink, then pulled a couple of beers from the 'fridge. The two men went out on the deck and sat down on a couple of wicker chairs.

Jigger padded behind them, tennis ball in mouth, and took a seat on Toby's outstretched foot. Toby regarded the dog for a few moments, then:

"Now why does he always plop his mangy butt on my shoes? —that can't be a comfortable spot for him!"

Belying his gruff tone, Toby scratched the dog behind his ears, eliciting a groan of pleasure from Jigger.

"He smells your shoes," Logan said with a shrug. "Must figure that's an appropriate place to park his butt."

The sun was a glowing cherry sinking into the ocean. This had been one of Ellen's favorite rituals, watching the sunset. The men sat in companionable silence, sipping beer and watching the sky change colors from shades of red to a mellow cinnamon. Logan never tired of the sight, though it was always bittersweet.   He somehow felt closer to her at these times.

"Thinking of her, huh?" Toby asked, taking a swig of his beer. He swallowed and let out a contented sigh.

"Silly question."

"I know. Me, too."

"*Everything* reminds me of her, Toby.   And I'm glad, even though it hurts."

"Well, in that case, I'll refrain from spouting off some philosophical bullshit to try to make you feel better."

"Thank you for that," Logan murmured.

When most of the colors had fled and the sun was a dying ember in the encroaching darkness, the oak and eucalyptus trees slowly blended together into one continuous, shadowy mass. A Screech-Owl announced its presence in the distance.

"Sounds a bit like Connie," Toby observed.

"Don't insult that poor bird," Logan scolded.

"Aw, go hug a tree."

The two sipped their beers and listened to the night sounds for a while.

Toby broke the silence. "What are you working on these days, buddy? Still trying to make your balls fly in that crazy do-dad of yours?" Toby grinned to punctuate his intentional omission of 'Ping-Pong' in the question.

"The word is levitate, not fly—and I did it!—at least for a while. Now I'm working on something else."

Toby must have caught something in Logan's voice. He leaned forward and said "Oh?"

Logan made a quick decision.   "I'll show you later, when you're done swilling all my booze."

Toby smirked, took a long pull of his beer, and then drawled, "It might be a while before the presentation, then."

"Trust me, pal, you'll be wanting to drink some more after you see it," Logan said, cryptically.

Toby paused, mid-sip, then completed the action. He gently placed the empty bottle on the porch rail and said:

"I see what you're trying to do here," Toby said with a sly edge to his voice. "You're thinking I'll become *sooo* curious that I'll stop at this one beer and follow you down to your shop.   Ain't gonna work, 'cause here's what's gonna happen."

Toby pushed up from his chair, went into the house and returned, laden with four more beers.

"Okay Dr. Frankenstein, let's go have a look at your latest creature."

"At least two of those better be for me, you swilling bum."

The two crunched down the graveled path to the shop.

Chapter III

Revelation

Toby echoed Logan's earlier sentiments:
"What the *hell* is that?"

A bottle of beer fell from his arms and shattered; amber puddle and broken glass going unnoticed.   Well, almost.

Jigger started to lap it up, but was absentmindedly nudged away by Logan.   Jigger liked all things fermented, hence his name—from the time he knocked over a Margarita pitcher and lapped up the contents before Ellen and Logan caught him. "Bart" became "Jigger" from that night on.

With the second go-to-hell look at his master that day, Jigger slouched over to his cushion, did a half-circle, and plopped down.

"Well?"

"You tell me, Toby.   I can tell you this: it isn't an image or hologram.   Things can be thrown into it, and pulled out. It's a portal to...somewhere."

Logan peered into the portal. It was night there, as well. Nothing else had changed, with the exception of a cloud drifting in that other-sky.

Toby edged a little closer to the oval.

"Looks a little like the Central Coast here—like the country North of Cambria," Toby observed.

"Yeah, it does, at that. Except I never saw grass and leaves moving that fast unless there was a gale-force wind behind them—but notice—the branches of the bushes aren't moving.   Freaky."

Toby stood in silence for a few beats, then:

"Okay, I admit you got me—it's a damn great prank, but how'd you do it? What do you have—some hidden mist machine and a projector somewhere?"

Toby looked from floor to ceiling for the alleged articles. He started to thrust his hand into the image when Logan grabbed his arm and shouted,

"No! It's not a trick! Don't touch it!"

Alarmed by his friend's reaction, Toby yanked his arm back as if stung, and took a step back.

Logan bent over, placed his hands on his knees and drew in a deep breath. Eventually, he looked up into his friend's startled face.

"It's no prank, Toby.   I don't know what the *hell* it is, but it...it's *real*. I have no idea what it might do to a living thing that...goes into it." Logan gave an involuntary shudder.

Toby gazed at Logan for a long period before speaking.

"You said, 'Objects can go into it...what objects? Show me."

After a moment's hesitation, Logan tore off a sheet of paper from the legal pad and wadded it up.   He handed it to Toby, and then swept his arm towards the anomaly in invitation.

Toby looked at the paper ball in his hand, then his eyes crinkled up in amusement and said,

"One small step..."

"Already said that.   Just throw."

"Oh," grunted a disappointed Toby, and he tossed the paper ball.

Before it could land in the grass, a large, black form streaked between the two men and leapt for the portal.

"Jigger, *no!*" Logan and Toby shouted in unison.

Jigger went through, landed awkwardly and skidded on his side, as if unprepared for the landing. He quickly bounded to his feet and snagged the paper ball.

"Jigger! Come back!" Logan shouted.   Jigger stood still and looked from side to side, ignoring the shout. His movements seemed quick and jerky.

Both men continued shouting for Jigger to return.   He eventually looked towards them, cocked his head to the side, and then began running back.

"Toby, he's going to come in hard and fast.   Brace yourself—we've got to catch him."

Toby gave Logan a quizzical look, but did as he was told—sliding his right leg back and redistributing his weight.

Jigger leaped, and then came through, striking the men with the force of a linebacker. They caught him, but were knocked to the floor.

"Jigger! Jigger, are you all right?" Logan gripped the dog by the ears. In answer, Jigger dropped a soggy paper ball in his master's lap.

As a relieved Logan buried his face in Jigger's fur, Toby sat back, one arm draped over his knee. He shook his head and chuckled.

"Well, I'll be fucked six ways to Sunday."

"Yeah, that about sums it up," Logan replied.

"Guess we both had it wrong, buddy," Toby drawled.

"What's that?" Logan looked up from Jigger's neck.

"It should be 'One small step for dog...'"

Both men sank to the floor, laughing.

Recovering, Logan said "Stupid, dumb-assed dog! You could have died!"

"But he *didn't*," Toby said, suddenly sober, "He *didn't* die—in fact, he seems to be completely unaffected."

"True," Logan answered, "but we have no idea what might have happened had he stayed there longer."

"From what I know—which is, admittedly, next to nothing—a toxic atmosphere would have had an immediate effect. Something. That wasn't the case, here."

"True, but still, this is the unknown—and that seems like a long leap of faith to me, Toby. What are you getting at?"

"Hell, Logan—you know as well as I what has to come next—*we have to go there!*"

"*We*? Toby—*we* don't even know where 'there' is! It could be anywhere...in the universe!"

"And it could be a few miles from here." Toby countered.

"Or *outside* of the universe. Toby, there are too many unanswered questions to try anything like that yet."

"Yet your dog lives," Toby climbed to his feet, "and he used the portal to get back."

Logan stabbed a finger at the portal. "Toby, I don't know how stable this thing is—hell, it could wink out of existence at any moment.   I made this by accident, and I'm not certain I could duplicate it."

"I'm just saying..."

"This could be a one-trick pony, for all we know. What would we do if it went away *while we were on the other side?* Think about it."

"Looks like you have." Toby sighed. "I see your point, though."

"I want like hell to go in there, too," Logan said, "but we need to take a few—no, a *lot*—of precautions, first."

"We could send those whirly-thingies," Toby twirled a long finger in the air, searching for the word "—drones! — We could send drones in to check out the area." Toby suggested, smacking a fist in his palm.

"I don't think remote control signals would work from here to the other side of the portal. Good idea, though. We could try. If that fails, we could go old school and activate cameras, hook 'em to balloons, and push them in there.

After a while, we could reel 'em back in, check out the pictures."

"Now we're cooking!" Toby shouted, rubbing his hands together in excitement. He reached out and slapped Logan on the shoulder.

Logan slightly staggered under Toby's enthusiasm—in more ways than one. He realized that he had to get control of the situation, quickly. He gripped Toby by the shoulders and looked him steadily in the eyes:

"Toby, I let you in on this because I trust you." Logan let the words hang for a couple of beats.

"We can't let anyone else know about this—not yet. Big Brother would descend on us like stink on shit and take it all away—and likely *us* as well.   This is *big*. We can't screw this up. If and when we report this, it will have to go very public—TV news crews, papers... the works—that way, it can't be hushed-up. Questions would then be asked if we were to suddenly disappear."

Toby remained silent for a while, stroking his chin. Logan expected to be accused of being paranoid.

"Yeah, I hear you," Toby said, after a few seconds. "You see, I used to work for Uncle Sam, and I know how all bets are off under the 'National Security' blanket. You can count on me with the hush-hush."

Logan was reminded that he knew very little about the life of his childhood friend after he and his family moved away, long ago. Toby wasn't big on talking about the intervening years; in fact he was downright evasive. When he returned, grown and with a few years experience under his belt, the two of them took up where they left off so many years ago.

When did he work for Uncle Sam?—and in what capacity? Logan knew he'd served a hitch or two in the

Navy, but sensed that there was more to the story.   Those questions were for later, though.

"I know I can trust you."

"But think of the *women* we could..."

"Toby...!"

"Just kiddin.' As long as you keep supplying me with beer."

"Goes without saying," Logan replied, grinning. "Let's get to figuring this out, shall we?"

* * *

The two friends worked well into the night, listing how the process of delving into the portal should be conducted. They dispensed with the beer and opted for hot coffee instead.

The first thing they would do is test to see if electrical signals could be transferred from one side of the portal to the other.

"What about that remote control car of yours, Logan? We could test this theory right now!"

"Do you know how much that thing costs? Are you crazy?"

Toby shrugged, holding his long arms out from his sides.

"All in the name of science, you know. Where are your priorities, anyway?" Toby said.

"No," Logan said firmly, with finality.

"But..."

"No! Damn it, Toby—Ellen gave me that car."

"Oh."

What would *Ellen have to say about it?* Logan thought, twirling a pencil between his fingers. *It could be her contribution to something that could change the course of human history.*

"All right. We'll do it."

"Naw, man—I didn't think, or I wouldn't have mentioned it. We'll buy something cheap at the toy store tomorrow and..."

"No." Logan said in a tone brooking no argument, "It's *because* it came from Ellen that I want to do it. It's her contribution to all of this. I want her in on it, Toby, as much as she can be, at least."

"Okay," Toby replied, "I guess she would have wanted it that way."

"Run home and get your video camera—that small camcorder," Logan said.

Dawning realization spread on Toby's face. "Oh, *hell* no, bro! That thing set me back a fortune and..."

"All in the name of science..." Logan mocked.

"Man, if this is some half-assed punishment for using your toy car—"

"It isn't," Logan cut him off. "My phone could be set on video, but I need it—it's my main source of communication. Your camcorder is small enough not to weigh down the car, and isn't something you need every day."

Toby grudgingly conceded to the logic of it and, grumbling, stepped out into the night.

"Just get your damned car ready!" he groused from the darkness.

Logan chuckled. He wanted Toby to make *some* contribution. Besides, if they couldn't recover either item, he'd give Toby the small camcorder he had, but neglected to mention.

An hour later saw a car/camcorder device—with copious amounts of duct tape—resting on a wooden ramp extending down into the portal.

"Once the car goes through, we'll test the remote from our side of the portal. If it works, we drive it around and film in every direction, then bring it back up the ramp."

"Riiiight…" Toby still seemed to rue the potential loss of his camcorder. Logan felt a flare of annoyance.

"Before we send it on its maiden voyage, though…do you have thirty dollars?"

Toby's brows joined together in a puzzled frown. "Why the hell do you need thirty dollars right now?"

"We could tape it to the camera, that way your investment would be more equal to my own."

Toby's eyes became slits, and he began to growl, "Kiss my sweaty, hairy a—"

"Here goes nothing…" Logan pushed the toggle and the car slowly made its way up the ramp. Logan slowed it down even more as it reached the nimbus.

"Why are you going so slow?" Toby asked, irritation still edging his voice.

"Just a hunch. Remember how Jigger seemed to move faster on the other side? I don't want the car to shoot down the ramp only to upend at the bottom."

"Yeah, I guess that's a good idea."

The car passed through the nimbus and accelerated for about a length and a half, and then stopped.

"Shit!" Toby pounded a fist on the worktable. "Well, at least it's close enough for us to stick something through and pull it back." Toby looked around the shop for the object to do just that.

"Wait, Toby." Logan pointed at the stalled car. "It's barely moving, but the tires are still rolling—look!"

The car continued at an almost imperceptible pace.

"It's probably just the slant of the board and gravity making it move," Toby said.

Logan kept peering at the car. "No, no. This car doesn't—can't—roll forward unless the gears are engaged. Something is interfering with the signal, but its still receiving it."

"Try backing it up," Toby suggested.

Logan reversed the toggle, but nothing seemed to happen, then:

"Yep, it's moving." Logan said.

"I don't see anything," Toby said, squinting at the car.

"See that imperfection in the board? Looks like a question mark? Use that as a marker."

Using the scratch as a point of reference, it became clear that the car *was* moving in the reverse, albeit at a snail's pace.

"Hot shit on a shingle, boy—it's slow as hell, but it's working!" Toby's teeth gleamed in a yard-wide smile.

The men exchanged a high five, then turned their attention back to the car/camera. They gaged its rate of progress down the ramp and determined that, all things remaining constant, the car would reach the bottom of the ramp in approximately forty minutes. Once at the end of the ramp, they would direct the car to move in a tight circle to film in all directions before bringing it back up the ramp.

Logan banged the cabinet with his fist. "We're so stupid, Toby! Why the hell didn't we tie a tether to the car before sending it down? That way, if it ran out of juice or tipped over, we could've at least pulled it back in!"

"I was wondering about that myself before sending it down, but I figured it was your show and you knew what you were doing," Toby said with a shit-eating grin.

"In other words, you're equally dumb-assed, but don't want to admit it."

"That's about it, more or less." Toby's shitty grin expanded.

His sense of humor has returned, at least, Logan observed.

"It's just that we're tired," Logan looked at the clock. "Shit—it's almost 2:00 a.m.! We should take a short cat nap while we're waiting."

"Great idea. I get the bed."

"You get the couch—if Jigger decides not to use it, that is."

At the house, Logan set his alarm and, surprisingly, managed to drift off to sleep before he was buzzed awake. Groggy but somewhat refreshed, he went into the living room. The creaking of the wood floor brought Toby wide awake.

"You're a jumpy little squirrel, aren't you?"

"It's kept my head attached to my neck so far," Toby returned.

Together, they set out in the chill night air for the shop again.

The car had made considerable progress.

"Hey, we called it pretty close, didn't we?" Toby said, "It's about five feet beyond the ramp, I'd say."

"It needs to get just a little further out before I put it in the tight turn. Don't want it ramming into the ramp," Logan said.

"So...what are you going to name it?" Toby asked.

"Name what?"

Toby rolled his eyes and swept his hand towards the portal. "Well this, ya ding-dong! I mean, you discovered it and all. Hell, for all we know, you might have even screwed up and *created* it!"

Logan laughed. "I think *you* are having delusions of my grandeur, pal.   For all we know, it's probably already called the Central Coast."

"Say it isn't...?" Toby wasn't letting it go.

"Well, then...I don't know. It looks a lot like our world...if it isn't, in *fact*, our world...like a twin."

"That's it? 'Twin'?" Toby's lip curled up in disdain.

"No." Logan thought of Ellen, and what she might have called it.

Ellen! Of course! He thought.

"Gemini," was Logan's somber proclamation.

"Gemini?—oh!" Toby caught on quickly. "For The Twins in the Zodiac! Classy—I like it."

And for Ellen, who was also a twin. Logan kept the thought to himself.

After the car had made sufficient progress past the ramp, Logan pushed the toggle and put the car in a tight, left-hand turn.

"Okay," he said, "I'm gonna set the alarm again for about...what do you think—an hour?—then I will send the car back up the ramp. Toby, you might as well go home and rest—it's going to take about two or three hours before it gets back up the ramp—that is, if the batteries last."

"I don't mind staying."

"Well, you're welcome to camp on my couch—or use one of the other bedrooms, but there isn't a hell of a lot either one of us can do but wait at this point. I know you put in a hard day's work already."

Toby sagged visibly, as if being reminded of it made his exhaustion suddenly real.

"I guess you're right. I've about had it. Call me as soon as that thing gets up the ramp. I want to see the photos with you."

"You got it, amigo," Logan clapped Toby on the shoulder and shook his hand. "When *I* see them, *you'll* see them."

Toby fired up his old truck and drove away. Logan turned and locked the shop. He set the alarm on his phone, and then headed back up to the house. He knew he couldn't sleep. Having to stay awake for at least three more hours, he decided to take a shower to help perk him up, as well as kill time.

After the shower, which helped immensely, he shaved. He observed his face in the mirror as he razed the stubble off his cheeks and jaw. How he had changed over the past two years! His grey eyes seemed shadowed and haunted, his cheek bones more prominent. His brown hair was in dire need of a trim. A tormented stranger stared back at him, someone he would rather not know, whom he wished he'd never met. This stranger silently spoke of tortured thoughts, loss, and anguish as he looked back at Logan.

Pulling his gaze from his face, he noticed that his frame was thinner. Though layered with muscle, he seemed gaunt. He'd been missing more than a few meals. Even Toby, who usually didn't ride his back, had pointed out that he should be taking better care of himself.

Whatever for? Logan thought. There were very few reasons, if any, he could think of—and that disturbed him. He wasn't suicidal...he simply didn't care. He stopped caring the day Ellen died.

His projects and experiments weren't only just a means to kill time and to pull him away from his misery; he was honestly curious, and yearned to learn more. He felt his thirst for knowledge was toward something specific, but he couldn't, for the life of him, determine what that was. Perhaps a purpose for continuing to live?

Finishing his bathroom rituals, he brewed a fresh pot of coffee. He took a can of mixed nuts from the pantry and ate a few handsful as he sipped coffee.

As was usually the case in those quiet moments alone in the dark, his thoughts turned inexorably towards the tragedy and chaos that was his life for the past two years.

* * *

Two Years Earlier

Logan's seven-months-pregnant wife, Ellen, was driving home from a checkup when a twenty-year-old college freshman, talking on her cell phone, swerved into her lane and drove her off the road. Her car rolled three times down an embankment before slamming into a stand of trees. Ellen and her unborn child died on impact.

The college student fled the scene, but other motorists gave a good description of her car and license plate. The girl later argued that Ellen's car was weaving, and went off the road on its own. Corroborating witnesses, however, negated her story. Further investigation proved that she had been talking to her boyfriend on the phone at the time of the accident.

The girl's father, a successful businessman, hired the best lawyers for his daughter. He demanded a toxicological report on Ellen's blood, claiming that she was somehow impaired at the time of the accident. He made statements to the press alluding to alcohol or drugs being present, but public opinion resolutely condemned both him and his unapologetic daughter. The toxicological report later proved that Ellen was not alcohol, or drug, impaired at the time of death.

Logan, at first bereaved and in shock, began to build hatred towards the girl and her family for the accusations and slander of his late wife. Though he knew nothing could bring Ellen and their unborn child back, the callous attitude of the girl and her family gradually filled him with rage. He wanted revenge.

During a recess in the trial, Logan sat midway down the long row of courthouse steps, collecting his thoughts and marshaling his emotions. The presiding judge stood near the courthouse entrance, taking in a breath of fresh air while watching with a baleful expression a small group of protesters.

An elderly woman emerged from the group and approached Logan.

"Sir?" she called, pulling Logan out of his dark reverie, "Young man, do you really think it serves you and your poor, deceased wife to destroy that little girl's life? Where is God's mercy in your heart?"

Logan's anger flared, but before he could respond, he was startled to silence when a voice boomed from behind him: "You get the hell away from him, madam, get away from him this instant or *I will have all of your asses thrown in jail!*"

Logan turned to see the judge storming down the courthouse steps, face purple and robe flapping in the breeze.

Spittle flew from the judge's lips as he raged. "I've never seen such callous, conniving, underhanded behavior in all my born days! You and your—group—will leave these premises immediately! Move!"

Police officers began appearing from out of nowhere, converging on the group which, in turn, dispersed posthaste. The woman stood for a moment with a hand fluttering over her heart, eyes wide and mouth working, before she almost ran down the courthouse steps. The judge spun around and stormed off into the courthouse without sparing a backwards glance. Doors boomed shut in his wake as he made his way back to his chambers.

Though he was not the recipient of the judge's wrath, Logan couldn't help but feel a bit intimidated himself by the display. He later learned that the woman and her group were members of the Savior's Grace Church, in which the girl's father was a deacon.

The judge, also lacking God's mercy, took the girl's license, gave her some jail time, and hit her (rather, her daddy) hard in the pocketbook with fines and an additional $3,000,000.00 judgment in favor of Logan. Logan couldn't have cared less about the money, but he was satisfied in knowing that the girl and her family suffered where it would hurt them the most—in the bank. A sincere apology and signs of remorse were all that he really wanted from them. Neither ever came, of course.

Chapter IV

Bean Time

"I know I've never seen those structures before, anywhere along the Central Coast," declared Toby.

Logan gazed at the images on the camera, freeze-framing the clearest shot—most of the rest were close-ups of nearby brush. In the background, there seemed to be several domed structures. It was a night shot—the time there seemed to be in sync with earth's, if in fact, it wasn't the same planet—so details and color were impossible to make out.

"Well, the Central Coast is a big place, Toby—just because *you've* never seen them doesn't mean they're not there."

"Aw, c'mon, Logan—how many domed structures like those are there around here? You haven't seen them either and, between the two of us, it seems damned unlikely that one of us hasn't seen them."

Logan made a placating gesture to his friend. "I know, I know—but think about it—is that concrete proof that this is another world?"

Toby sighed and plopped on a stool. "I suppose you're right."

"And, not to burst your *second* bubble, we can't really tell if these are artificial structures or part of the landscape."

Toby cocked an eyebrow. "Really? You've seen perfect domes like that in nature? Give me a break." Toby reached for the camera.

"I agree—I'm almost a hundred-percent sure that these aren't natural, but science demands absolutes."

Toby guffawed. "Now *that* last statement is the biggest bunch of bullshit I've heard coming out of your mouth. Dude, science is almost *nothing* but theory." Toby ticked a list off with his fingers. "Gravity is a theory. Evolution is a theory. Black Holes are a theory. Tell me something out there that has been proved beyond a shadow of a doubt by science."

"Okay: the Sun is the center of the solar system. Earth isn't flat."

"Hah! There are still people who would argue *that* hasn't been proven beyond a doubt. Remember old Mrs. Hale? *She* claimed the earth was flat and the moon landing was a bunch of made-up bullshit! She was a pretty wise gal in most respects."

"She also claimed that, if you left a horse hair in a jar of water long enough, it would turn into a worm," Logan added, laughing at the memory.

"My point is this: could you, by yourself, prove her wrong? *Nothing* can be proven absolutely to *all* people. Some of today's cutting-edge scientific theories will be tomorrow's quaint and funny wives' tales."

Seeing he had no argument to give, Logan conceded with a chuckle.

Toby swiped through the different shots, then quietly said "Holy shit."

"What?" Logan felt adrenaline course through his veins at the expression on Toby's face.

"Well," Toby drawled as he handed the camera back to Logan, "it sure as shit ain't the Central Coast."

Logan looked at the image and saw *two* moons in the night sky. A second and third frame showed the same thing.

"I'd say you're right, Toby." Logan shifted his gaze from the camera to the portal. "I'd say you're right."

* * *

Discovering that the portal led to another world did little to answer the crucial questions about how to deal with the anomaly. Logan had a difficult time keeping Toby from simply tying a rope around his torso and plunging through the portal. Truth be told, he had a hard time keeping himself from doing the same thing. The fact that Jigger had spent some time on the other side, albeit a brief time—and lived—only made it that much more tempting. Logan thought of Tantalus, the ancient king punished by the gods to be forever unable to drink the water at his feet, or eat the fruits within his reach. Knowing that they were a step away from another world—and *not* going to said world— was an exquisite torture.

"Buddy, I hear you when you say you want to be cautious, but remember, there's such a thing as being over-cautious as well." Toby had a look of intense yearning as he stared into the portal.

"Look, Toby, I want to go there as much as you—maybe more, if that's possible—but I want to have a few safeguards in place first. I want to test the atmosphere, for one thing…"

"But Jigger…"

"… was there for only a few seconds. Hell, I can survive in a toxic environment for a few seconds. We need to make a few simple tests, first.   Also, I need to round up components to make an exact copy of this portal, and a power source, for the other side."

"Why the hell do you need that? You already have a doorway."

"What if we're over there on the other side and the power goes out here for some reason? We'd be marooned on a strange planet in God-knows-what quadrant of the universe—if it *is* in this universe."

"Well, true enough—you can only trust the electric company so far. By the way, are you paid up on your utility bill?" Toby chuckled halfheartedly.

"Yeah, unless the check bounced—then we're screwed. I want to get back-up power for this shop, too—just in case."

Toby ran a hand through his unruly, black hair. "Guess we should start making a list. I've probably got more knowledge of what we'll need for basic survival, with my military background. I'll make a list of the necessities."

"Now you're talking. And I'll get a list together of the things we'll need for experiments, power sources, and stuff like that."

"Should we set a time-line on when we're ready to step into the Great Unknown?"

"We'll need a solid two months, at least." Seeing Toby's stricken expression, he added "Sorry."

"Oh, I'm like a reckless kid with this. No need to be sorry." Toby sighed. "What's the point of going on a great adventure, if we don't live to tell about it?"

The two men got busy and made their lists, comparing and adding a few things. Days, then weeks, flew by with the planning, purchasing, and fabrication. Toby did prove the best choice for getting survival gear, thinking of situations that Logan didn't take into account.

"You ever think that maybe something from *that* side might decide to see what life is like on *this* side?" Toby mentioned one day, "Maybe something that we don't want to meet in this little shop?" It was Toby who suggested that they make a Plexiglas shield surrounding the portal.

The two men constructed the large box with a sealed, locking door. They slipped it over the anomaly and bolted it to the floor. They reinforced it with steel straps at the top and bottom, tightened with a come-along and welded in place.

When they finished, Toby gave it an experimental shake. "Well, it's sturdy enough to keep us out, in any event."

Logan thought to suspend a motion sensing camera from the ceiling so that, if they were gone from the shop for an extended period of time, they could review the film to see if there were any changes.

One day, as they reviewed the footage, they saw movement in the distance, but were unable to determine what it was. Even so, both men were excited to see the first signs of life there, other than plant life.

The shield and the camera proved to be invaluable, allowing the men more free time to prepare and not feel the need to constantly monitor the portal.

"We make a pretty good team, you know it?" Logan remarked to Toby one day.

Toby grinned. "Sure—you to get your dumb ass in a sling, and me to pull it out."

"This coming from the man who wanted to tie a rope around his waist and jump into another world. Yeah, you're the level-headed one of the pair, Toby." Logan punctuated his remark by bouncing Jigger's dirty tennis ball off Toby's forehead.

Toby lunged for the ball to return the favor, but Jigger reclaimed it first and ran away.

"Harsh! Dissed by the dog!" Logan roared a laugh. "You just relax and let me and Jigger do all the thinking from now on." Logan walked briskly away when Toby stooped to pick up a rock.

A month and a half later saw Logan and Toby standing in the workshop, going over checklists and sorting through supplies. They had spent over $40,000.00 purchasing materials and supplies. The sheer volume of items purchased threatened to take up all of the space in the workshop, until Toby had another brilliant idea:

"Hell, we have the largest storage room in the universe."

Logan cocked an eyebrow at his friend. "Do tell."

Toby pointed at the portal. "We can throw a lot of the stuff in there—that's where it's going, anyway, right?"

They spent most of an hour going over the pros and cons of the idea. Logan, having spent a small fortune on the items, did not much cotton to the idea of putting them in a place in which they may never be recovered.

"You *are* planning on going over there to explore, aren't you? I mean, that *was* the whole point of all this."

"Yeah, but..."

"But nothing. It's about time we put up or shut up."

Logan agreed. He did demand that the stuff be camouflaged before being thrown in the portal. Two dirt bikes, tents, tools, water filters, etc., were soon lying haphazardly on the surface of another world.

Logan wore a mournful expression on his face as he observed the pile of stuff.

"My God, Toby—" Logan indicated the pile "—is this how we foreshadow our arrival on another world? That looks like a damn trash-heap!"

Toby clapped him on the shoulder. "Yeah, but it's an *expensive* damn trash-heap. Whoever might discover it will surely take that into account."

"Another thing—despite the camo covering, all that stuff stands out. It could be spotted by someone—or something—from miles away."

Toby stood regarding the pile of goods for a few moments before saying "Nah," and turning back to his inventory work.

Logan, annoyed at Toby's lack of concern, flipped the clipboard over his shoulder and stalked off with Toby's words trailing him:

"No sense in wasting time and energy worrying about something you can't do anything about." Toby added insult to injury by chuckling softly.

He may be right, Logan thought, *but* God!—*why does he have to be such an ass about it?*

SECTION TWO

Debra Davis Hinkle

Dedication

Dedicated to the man who didn't get away, Roland Boothe Hinkle—thanks for the forty plus years that you have filled my life with love and laughter.

Thanks to Joshua David Baker and Kyle Taylor Murphy, the other men in my life. You will never know just how wonderful it is, for me, to be your Aunt.

With gratitude to my mother, Betty Davis, for so many things: sharing her love of animals, gardening, and teaching me about God—which was more like showing me what a good woman was.

Special thanks to the Friday Night Writers' Group, past and present members for their invaluable critiques and long friendships: Shirley Radcliff Bruton, Jim Leonard, B. Carter Pittman, Destry Ramey, Christine Taylor, Susan Tuttle, and Laurie Woodward.

Author's Bio

Author, poet, and artist, Debra Davis Hinkle grew up in Manhattan Beach, California, and currently lives in San Luis Obispo with her husband. She loves animals and has seven cats (three are feral), and a German shepherd. She is the godmother of *Binx Pittman*.

She graduated with a Bachelor of Science from California State University, Long Beach, in Business with emphasis in Information Systems. She has taught computer classes, built websites, and was the past Webmaster for SLO NightWriters.

Debra has been writing for fourteen years. She specializes in creative non-fiction and has numerous awards, including the Lillian Dean First Page Contest several times and The SLO NightWriters Short Story contest.

Her short stories have been published in Tales from the Corner, an anthology, published by Central Coast Press. Debra's poems have been published in the Tribune and Women's Press.

Debra co-authored a book on bereavement in 2013. She has two – three books coming out in 2018. Her work is available at www.amazon.com.

Debra is a founding member and leader of the Friday Night Writers' Group—a writing critique group started in 2008.

IT'S NOT A DREAM

This nightmare from Hell starts with a sharp twinge in my left side. Ouch! It escalates with a potent jolt. Another stab makes me swallow my first painkiller. The knife twists a little as I think about the nine-hundred-dollar co-pay for an emergency room visit. In waxing pain, I down my second pill. An ice pick jab ends my concern about a co-pay. Shaking, I hit the speed dial for my husband.

"Another kidney stone!"

"I'll be right there," he says.

"How long is right there?"

Sweating and shaking in misery, I enter the emergency room. My teeth, initially gritted, chatter as I linger for the doctor.

"Pain ki-ki-killer?"

"As soon as your IV is hooked up," the doctor responds.

I guess the doctor is blind, or I just imagined the IV hookup already in my left hand. A pain relief cocktail enters my vein, finally. The drugs cause a dream-like state, and I don't feel the usual claustrophobia when I have a CT scan.

"The test results show a three-millimeter stone that's sitting at the bladder junction. I'm sure you won't have any more problems. We're sending you home," the doctor announces without hesitation.

Nine hours later, screaming like a banshee, I enter the hospital for the second time in one day. My hair and nightgown are sweat-soaked. Wrenching in agony until the merciful medications hit me. Dreamland lasts for twenty minutes till the drugs wear off. Again, I must wait the excruciating seconds until more arrives.

"Get this thing out of me. Now!"

This piece won second place in the Lillian Dean First Page Writing Competition and the SLO NightWriters Short Story Contest in 2009.

THE BISCUIT MAKER

No
chattering
growling
hissing.

Only
meowing
cooing
purring.

Whiskers forward
pacing back and forth
marching up and down.

Toes divided
claws extended
pulling the threads of the
white down comforter.

The biscuit maker
makes his kneads known.

SHE'LL BE YOUR BEST FRIEND

I'm four years older than my sister. While I am rather demonstrative, my sister is introverted. Usually, it's the older sister who is annoyed by the pesky younger sister. However, when the elder sister has Attention Deficit Hyperactivity Disorder (ADHD), that brings a whole new definition to the word "pesky," and that changes the normal big sister-little sister relationship. It creates an upside-down world when the older sister becomes the annoying one.

Photo: Debra and her sister

I've finally come to treasure the differences between us. It's taken me a very long time to appreciate that she doesn't talk rapidly or a lot.   When she has something to say, she will say it, so I better be listening very carefully.

Since our mother died, six years ago, my sister has tried twice to tell me a story from our childhood, but because of the ADHD I missed what she was trying to tell me, both times. The tale goes something like this:

"Mom, when is Debby going to stop driving me crazy?" Donna asked for the umpteenth time.

"Just wait until you grow up, she'll be your best friend," Mom said as she glanced at her very petite kindergartener.

Recently, I finally heard it; that was my sister's way of saying "I love you, and you are my best friend."

Mom, you were right, after all, and at least one of us was listening the first time, too.

DINNER EVERY THURSDAY

Mommy and I are in the kitchen together. Our rectangular-shaped yellow Formica table gets lost in the big dining room. I helped Mommy make yellow-checked curtains for the three big windows. She is cooking dinner, and I am playing hopscotch on the deep brown tiles—I never miss when throwing my chain into the sixth square, even on the slippery linoleum. "Mommy, can I draw the ten's circle with chalk?"

"No, your dad would kill us both."

"Mommy, do I look like you?"

"Yes, Honey! You have dark curly hair and so do I, but I have blue eyes. My skin is a little darker than yours, too."

"What color eyes do I have?"

"Your eyes are hazel."

"What color is hazel?"

"Your eyes are light brown in the center and green around the edge. They are rare and lovely, Honey—just like you."

"Oh." I like looking like my mommy, because she's beautiful, and I love her a lot.

I know it is Thursday, because I can smell stinky liver and onions. If it were Wednesday, we would be having spaghetti, and if it were Friday, we would be having pigs-in-a-blanket. Pigs-in-a-blanket smells worse than liver and onions but doesn't taste quite as yucky. "Mommy, why can't we have something to eat that I like?"

"Your dad wouldn't like it if I changed the weekly menu that he sets for us."

"But I hate liver and onions."

"I know, Honey."

"Mommy, when I turn eight, can I have what I want for dinner?"

"I will ask your dad, but don't count on it," her voice trailing off. "Go play in your room until he gets home." I skip to my room, my curls bouncing all the way.

I quickly put away my jacks when I hear my dad come through the front door. Dad is very tall and thin. His hair is dark and very short—it sticks straight up in a "crew cut." He has very light skin, but it looks dark because he always needs a shave when he comes home. I don't know what color his eyes are because I'm afraid to look at them.

Dad is an engineer, and he wears the same thing every day to work—a white shirt, dark tie and pants, white socks and black shoes. Dad's shirt has plastic in the pocket. He has a mechanical pencil that writes in four colors and a slide rule hanging out of his plastic pocket. I like to color with the fancy pencil, but Dad spanked me the last time I touched it. I don't know what a slide rule is, and it looks neat, but I'm not going to touch it.

"I'm home," Dad yells as he heads for the bathroom to get washed up for dinner.

"Dinner's ready," Mommy says.

"Girls, line up and wash your hands for dinner," Dad says.

Dad is standing guard at the bathroom door as I exit with my washed hands tucked safely behind me.

"Show me your hands, young lady. Can't you do anything right? Do you need me to wash your hands?"

"No! No! I'll do it again." I can hear the conversation coming from the dinner table over the running water.

"Daddy, when are we going to eat?" my nine-year-old sister, Linda, asks.

"We will eat when Debby finally finishes cleaning her dirty hands." *How come I always must wash my hands twice, but my sisters only have to wash their hands once?*

Like always, I am the last to the table. At least, I get to sit next to Mommy out of range of my angry dad's hands. The light from the windows makes the dining room area very bright; but very soon it will get as dark as the brown linoleum tiles.

Dad prays, "Dear Lord, bless our food and make us ever mindful of those who are less fortunate."

I pray my silent prayer now. *Dear Lord, help me to not gag too much or throw up.*

Dad fills everyone's plates. I think he always gives my sisters less than me when it's something I don't like. Pam, Linda, and Donna never complain about the food or how much he serves them. Maybe I'm the only one who hates liver and onions. Tears form in my eyes as I watch in slow motion as my plate disappears under the liver and onions. But, I know better than to cry. If I could only say "No thank you," or "None for me, please." It doesn't really matter what I would say, because Dad would just smack me.

First, I try hard to pretend I'm eating most of my meal. Slowly, I cut the tough liver into little pieces and then try to hide them under the fried onion sauce. I can't hide it all. Next, I have to put some of it in my mouth. *Yuck.* The first little piece makes my stomach ache. I pretend to cough and spit the piece out in my napkin. This works pretty well. I do this for a few times and then my paper napkin is full. *Why didn't I think to put some extra napkins in my pockets?*

I am at the point I dread every week. I don't know any more tricks. I have to really chew and swallow that *icky* stuff. It's thick, tough and difficult to chew. I would rather chew the bottom of my old Ked shoe—I bet it would even taste better. I gag. I always gag.

Now, all eyes *seem to be* on me. And here it comes. "Get under the table and take your plate with you."

"Okay." Tears fall as I slither between my chair and the table, but I don't have to stop them now. I lean against my Mommy's leg. She is warm, and she doesn't try to kick me. I feel safer now, and I don't feel sick to my stomach anymore.

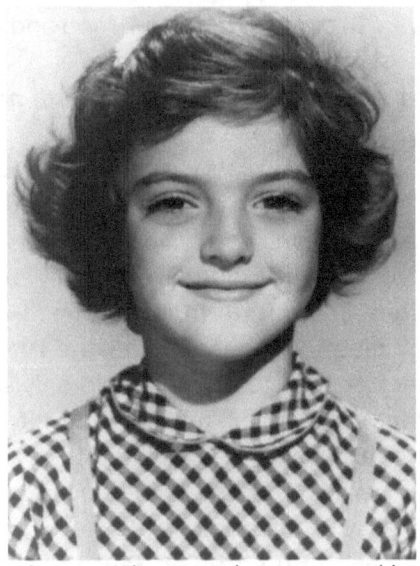

Photo: Debra around seven years old

* * *

Even though I have three sisters they don't play with me—I don't even get to share their bedroom—I must stay in my own small room. I feel left out and so I have an imaginary friend, Kaye. After a while, I ask her to sit under the table with me. Kaye tells me it's not so bad under the table and promises to stay with me.

Kaye says, "My daddy doesn't make me eat stuff I hate." Kaye and I play very quietly waiting for my dad's voice to rise again.

And when everyone has finished dessert, Dad says, "Get to your room and stay there the whole night. And, I better not catch anybody talking to her for the rest of the evening," warning my sisters and mother. I put my plate on the sink, and Kaye and I go to my room.

Much later, I hear my mommy come into my room very quietly.   Mommy whispers, "I brought you a peanut butter sandwich and some milk. Honey, after you are done eating, hide the glass under your bed and don't forget to put your paper napkin in your glass."

"Mommy, am I a bad girl?"

"No, Debby."

"Then why doesn't Dad love me?"

"He loves you, Honey, in his own way."

"I don't understand."

"Honey, just eat and go to sleep."

I share my sandwich and milk with Kaye because she didn't get to eat either.

Later, I pray, *Dear Lord, make me a better girl so my dad will love me.* Kaye prays too—*Dear Lord, make Debby's dad more like my dad.*

FADING FUR COAT

Scan QR code to listen to poem.

Found you twelve years ago.
Leader of your colony.
Thought you fearsome—
strength and stamina
strong hind muscles
built for instant speed
savage carnivore.
A wild being
in a marmalade colored fur coat.

Years later
I know you are
tame with a feral streak.
How proud you are
when you bring me gifts of
mice, rats, snakes, gophers and rabbits.
A sweet old boy
in a fading marmalade colored fur coat.

Photo: Big Boy resting in the backyard

FATHER

<u>Scan QR code to listen to poem.</u>

While I was still in diapers
you taught me to fear
your cruel touch.
Later, I grew to hate you
and
mistrust all males.

Much later, I pitied you
and
friends taught me to discern
good from bad men.

Uncle Bob's love
and the long friendship with
two writers:
Jim Leonard and Carter Pittman,
taught me that
men can be good.

* * *

While growing old,
with a wonderful man,
I was finally
able to forgive you.

* * *

It would have been
so much easier,
if you had
just been
a good father.

Photo: Debra around three years old holding her sister's fish

IT CAME ANYWAY

Blood he drew
didn't make him stop,
beating my little body
curled up tightly to look small.

Pain he caused
didn't come back to haunt him,
as I prayed to God, it would—
so, I would know he suffered, too.

Forgiveness he didn't deserve,
and I was unable to give,
came anyway—
after putting him in a nursing home
and closing the door.

A LANGUAGE ALL THEIR OWN

The leaves on the maple trees that line the parkway on my mother's street are turning hues of red, orange and yellow. They circle in the breeze, sometimes landing on the ground, and others fly away to unknown destinations. It's both pleasing and messy, but not unusual for an autumn day in Canyon Country—a large city in the northernmost part of Los Angeles County. The outside beauty is just a prelude to what is behind the door. I can't wait to see my mom and two nephews.

"Mom, I'm finally here."

"How was the traffic, honey?"

"Awful! Where are the boys?"

"Outside. Boys, Aunt Debby's here!"

The boys knock me over as I ask, "Where are my hugs and kisses?"

"Aunt Debby, do you want to play?"

"Maybe later. Right now, I would like to talk to your grandmother and just watch my two favorite boys play."

"Okay!   Kyle, let's go back outside."

Mom and I chat occasionally, but mostly we watch and listen to my sister's two young boys playing in the backyard. The backyard has a small patio—maybe eight by ten feet with a wood slat cover letting in rays of sunlight and warmth all day. On one side of the patio is a cement walkway, and on the other side is a very small dirt area where the boys are playing under the only tree in the yard.

Photo: Josh and Kyle

Josh appears at the screen patio door, "We're hungry."

"Oh. Mom, what can I give the boys to eat?"

"You could heat up some SpaghettiOs, or there's cheese and crackers in the pantry."

"Josh, what do you want?

"I'll have SpaghettiOs, and Kyle wants cheese and crackers. Can we eat outside?"

"If it's okay with Grandma, then it's okay with me."

"Grandma, can we—"

"—Yes, you can eat outside."

"I'll bring lunch outside when it's ready, Josh." Fifteen minutes later, I set their lunch on the picnic table. "Boys, lunch is ready." Josh is on his third bite as I lift Kyle up to the table.

Back inside, I watch my nephews eat and share their food. You wouldn't know they were brothers, except for the little freckles across their noses and the color of their eyes—bluish green with green halos. The little one is pudgy, his hair is straight as a stick, and he can't talk yet. He is demanding and opinionated; he grunts to make himself known. This works quite well for Kyle so far. The big brother is slim with very curly hair. And, although he can talk, Josh is quiet by nature. He is kind and easy going. Josh gives Kyle his way on most things so there is little fighting between them.

When they continue playing with Hot Wheel cars in the dirt under my mother's peach tree, I eavesdrop on their utterances. A short grunt means "yes" or "okay" and a longer deeper grunt means "no" or "don't." The boys don't seem to need a two-way verbal conversation; it is good enough the way it has always been.

"Kyle, I want to be tall like Uncle Roland. I don't want to be short like my dad. Kyle, don't you think it's better to be tall?"

Short grunt.

"Let's build a bridge. Where would you like it? Right here?"

Longer and deeper grunt.

"Over here?"

Short grunt.

"I'll build the bridge and you watch."

Short grunt.

And, so goes another wonderful quiet afternoon watching and listening to precious moments. What I wouldn't give to stay here a little longer!

"Kyle, would you like Auntie to stay longer?"

Short grunt.

THE GRACIOUS LADY

The sweetest rose in all the garden; how did I ever get so lucky to get you as my Mom?" I dedicated these words to my mother-in-law, Melrose, on my first published work in December 2005. I was happy and proud to give her the book.

Just a few months later, the day before my birthday, she was gone. Mom was ninety-two, and most people would say she lived a long and full life. That's true, but I'm still going to miss her.

It was just a twist of fate and grief that my husband's idea of celebrating my birthday was to pack up Mom's room. So, there I was, sorting through her clothes, feeling sad but determined to finish cleaning up her things.

I took a break and thought I would share the book's dedication with Mom's caregiver. However, it was her caregiver who shared a heart-rending story with me—one I will never forget.

She began her story with "Melrose loved Debby," not knowing that I was Debby—the person who had dedicated the book to Mom. She told me that Mom slept with the book on her chest every night. The caregiver was just telling me something she thought was touching about Melrose, my mother-in-law, "The Gracious Lady."

And, then I felt I heard a voice saying, "Happy Birthday, *Dear.*"

Photo: Melrose in her kitchen

I WANT MY MOMMY!

Scan QR code to listen to poem.

Whenever I'm sick,
I always want my mom.
It doesn't matter how
old I am
or
what is wrong with me.

I want my mom,
just because.
What she couldn't make better
she made bearable.

This poem was published in the SLO Tribune in April 2017.

ROBIN EGGS

Bite off
outer colored shell,
expose malt.

Wave it
under her nose.
Raspy tongue—
lick, lick, lick.
Malt gone.

No need to
wave a second one.
Old Girl begs
for next and next.

She loves them.
Do all cats?

Photo: Pumpkin (Old Girl) resting on our deck

LOOKING FOR A GRANDMA

When my nephew, Kyle, was ten, he lost both of his grandmothers. This is a conversation we had after he heard me talking about my mother-in-law.

Photo: Kyle's Grandmother

"Aunt Debby, am I related to Uncle Roland's mom?" Kyle asked.

"No honey."

"She's not like my grandma, too?" Kyle inquired.

"She could be your grandma, if you wanted her to be. But, she's getting up there in years." I responded.

"How old is she?"

"She's eighty-nine."

"How old was Grandma when she died?"

"She was only seventy-five."

"Oh! I guess she's too old to be my grandma!" Kyle sadly concluded.

I know the feeling of loss and looking around to fill the void. I guess he couldn't risk another imminent loss. I know that feeling, too.

RED HOT PEPPER

From the day we met,
that was us—
one red hot pepper—
never two.

Shiny and new
for twenty-five years.
Then a big knife
cut us in two.

Where's the Super Glue?

    * * *

Oh my God,
the Super Glue worked.
And it was on sale.

One red hot pepper,
again.

IT'S NOT PERSONAL

It's not personal to whom?   It's certainly personal to me.   Remember, if it feels personal, it probably is personal.

Logic tells me the person knew that they did something that someone took personally.

The phrase reminds me of a non-apology apology.   The person isn't apologizing; they are making a statement to someone who has been offended that sounds as if they are sorry.

Borrowing from a famous literary character, Hercule Poirot, I think I'll use "my little gray cells" to decipher this preposterous verbalism.

Let's listen closely: "It's not personal" or "I'm sorry you took it that way." Neither statement makes you feel as if they are genuinely sorry—they just want you to think they're sorry. Compare those two statements to: "I'm so sorry." There is no comparison, to me—one is two oranges and the other is an apple.

In my opinion, a compassionate and empathetic human being would stop the behavior and apologize: "I'm sorry" or "Forgive me; I didn't mean to hurt you."   Those are real and sincere apologies of a human being trying to mitigate the damage to, or pain of, another person.

I doubt that Hercule Poirot would need to run this statement through his "little gray cells" again, and I know I don't. I recognize a phrase being used to justify past, present and future bad behavior, cruelty or lack of empathy. I think Hercule would conclude that the statement is false and say something like, "Does he really think Poirot is so stupid as to not see the absurdity and insincerity in that phrase?"

I'm not sure how two other famous literary characters, Sherlock Holmes or Dr. Watson, might respond to such a statement, but I want to say "Bullshit," and then ask them, "Does anyone believe that?"

In polite company, maybe I should just do the one hundred-yard dash the next time I hear "It's not personal." I could sincerely yell, "It's not personal" as I was haulin' ass.

Reductio ad absurdum (Assertion is false because of its absurdity.)

MY BEST FRIEND AND TEACHER

Some things were easy to instruct:
beading and needlepoint,
sewing and knitting,
baking, but not cooking.

Other things were best shown, not taught:
the difference between right and wrong,
never swearing.
I got right and wrong, but damn, I missed swearing.

Along the way, my teacher instilled in me:
honesty, empathy and kindness,
a great love of all animals—
especially cats.

Some of her favorite words to me:
"Look before you leap."
"Just because so and so does it…"
"I know you'll always tell me the truth."

My teacher taught me how to garden and arrange flowers,
to appreciate and collect Depression glass.
She trained me in art of Christmas shopping,
before and after.

She tutored me about God and heaven.
Faith I had to learn the hard way,
after she was gone.

She was a great friend and teacher.
Her frequent lesson—
patience,
finally learned during her last illness—
Cancer—
took her just six years ago.

I miss you, Mom.
But, you're still teaching me.

Hinkle, Debra Davis, and Jim Leonard. Tears to Laughter: Embracing the Future Without Forgetting the Past, Page 163. Dac Says Publishing, 2013.

THE RING

My mother's
ruby red ring
encircles my
finger,
my life, my dreams
and all that I am.

The stone is
diamond faceted underneath
and an unusual
combination cut on top.
Its beauty
binds us together,
then and now.

When I was little
I played with her ring
on and off her finger—
spinning it round
both our fingers

Now that she is gone,
those memories
comfort me.

Its intense, red color,
faceting and size
make me
think of her, still.
A day never goes by
that I would not trade
this ring for her.

When I was twenty-five,
Mom gave her ring to me.
When I was fifty,
and Mom was dying,
I gave it to my sister.
Fourteen years later
she gave it back.

It's a family thing—
this ring of ours.

Photo: *Mom bought this ring in 1944*

NEMO

He is
always able
and ready; wait-
ing so close by.
Just barely touch-
ing.   He never
barks or bites.
There is no ball,
bone, or bowl; only
the job of seeing for
his master. He lets out a
slight rumble, then gets
a gentle stroke. Ultimately,
he gives a wet lick.   He
readjusts position and then
        set-   tles back down.   He is
    al-   ways hopeful; he wants
     to   guide.   He is a seeing
   eye   dog.   "Guide you now?"

This is called a shape, concrete, or pattern poem. It is also sometimes called visual poetry.
The typographical effect (shape) of it is more important in communicating the meaning than the words.

THE DIAMOND

A lesson in envy and love.

On my first trip to my boyfriend's parents' home, his mother starts a conversation about a diamond that she bought from her brother, an assayer for a mining company in Arizona. I think the conversation is a little unusual for our first visit, but maybe it's just on her mind or the diamond is still new to her.

"Would you like to go with me to see the diamond?"

"I'd love to see it. I like jewelry."

"Okay, let's go to the safety deposit box tomorrow morning."

"Sounds good to me. How far is the bank?"

"Not too far. Everything is close in Coronado."

I wonder why my boyfriend's mother wants to show me her diamond—and why it's in her safety deposit box.   But, I am uncomfortable asking those whys and the biggest why—why are you showing it to me?   Did she know that her son and I have been talking about marriage—well, I've been talking and he's listening—I think?

How big is this diamond? What shape is it? Is it a loose stone?... I think, tomorrow would bring some answers to those questions, and maybe others, too.

The next morning, we head for the bank. It surprises me that she's taking a stranger to her bank, but I keep my mouth closed. *I wonder if she knows my mother was a Sunday School teacher when I was little. Maybe, she's just very trusting.*

"We're here."

I follow her inside the bank and then through the gate and finally to the vault. She takes the safety deposit box into a very small room and I follow her. I just watch as she pulls out a velvet pouch with draw strings and opens it.

"Do you like it?"

"It's..." My mouth is hanging open, but I have no words. After what seems like a minute, but was probably only a few seconds, I manage to say, "It's stunning," all the time thinking, *it's the biggest damn diamond I will ever see.*

"Do you think I should have it set into a ring?"

"Absolutely, and soon, too. You got this from your brother?"

"Oh, no honey, we paid five-hundred dollars for it."

"Oh. I'm not passing judgement or trying to pry; the size surprises me." Finally, I ask, "How big is it?"

"A little over two carats."

"That's a-a-a nice size stone." But I am thinking, *that's a gargantuan rock.* I'm still wondering why she's showing me the diamond. Is there something I don't know? I hope so.

Then it is over. The diamond goes back in its little black velvet container, back in the safety deposit box and finally she locks the box with two keys. The diamond is gone. But not forever.

She drives us back to their house, and as soon as I can get my boyfriend alone I ask, "Roland, why is your mother showing me that diamond?"

"I don't know."

"Do you think it's strange to show it to your girlfriend, that she just met the day before?"

"Well, maybe."

"I think it's strange and I can't help wondering why." There's that *why* again.

The next time I see the diamond, my mother-in-law has been widowed and is wearing the rock set in a filigree-cut yellow gold ring. I thought it big when I saw it in the bank, but it is enormous set in a ring.

Her ring. Not mine. That answers the nagging question. Darn.

I guess there isn't any special reason she shows it to me, either.

I don't have a diamond; I have a two-carat fake. A very nice imitation, but... My husband and I don't buy an engagement ring and instead we put a down payment on an investment piece of property just before we are married. It is an extremely practical thing to do. But, sometimes I ask myself, "Where's my diamond?" and then I answer, "It's down the street and over a block." The internal conversation never changes.

"Do you like it?"

"Wow. I love it. It's beautiful," I say, with just a touch of jealousy. Well, maybe a little more than a dash. I want that diamond. Her diamond.

Over the years, I often see the diamond—every holiday, and we spend the first week of September vacationing at her house every year. Sometimes she will visit us, or my husband's brother, and all the family will get together. The diamond always comes with her.

At first, she wears the dazzling stone on her right ring finger. Later when arthritic changes affected her joints, the rock moves to her left ring finger and her wedding set shifts to her smallest digit on her left hand.

My husband and I talk about the visit to the bank and the viewing of the ring occasionally over the years. The bank visit continues to confuse me. At least I was able to voice the disappointment when I figured out that she isn't giving it to me. It made sense at the time. It's a little funny, too, but only after many years.

I've eyed that exquisite diamond for more than a quarter century. When my mother-in-law enters a care facility and stops wearing the ring. She passes it on to her youngest son, my husband, and he will never wear a pinky ring or any other kind of diamond ring.

And, this is where my hope starts all over again.   God how I love that diamond—and I want it.   Maybe he would give it to me for my birthday or our twenty-fifth wedding anniversary next year.

That birthday comes and goes.   Maybe he doesn't know how much I want it. How can I let him know?   Should I tell him I want it, or just ask for it? I don't know of a way to hint for it.

I want that diamond.

That anniversary comes and goes, too.   No diamond— not for me anyway.   It is hard for me not to be upset and I feel guilty for my desire of the stone.

What is he waiting for—his mother's death?

And, then she is gone, and the diamond isn't important next to the loss of her. For a long while, anyway.

Our thirtieth anniversary is near.   And, I'm hopeful again—more than hopeful.   I'm desperate for that damn diamond. Why do I want it so much? What is so great about a rock?   I can't answer these questions.   I couldn't understand my deep wanting of the stone, and I sure as hell couldn't understand why he wouldn't give it to me.

We were married thirty years last month.

* * *

There are so many adjectives to describe a diamond, but the lasting ones: *reflecting, illuminating* and *shining* are the three that stick with me.

I've done a lot of reflecting over the years about my desire for the stone and the losses our family has faced. That reflection has been very painful yet illuminating.

I wear my husband's ring occasionally and I'm always aware that I would easily give up the stone to see the beautiful blue eyes and smile of my sweet mother-in-law, Melrose Peterson Hinkle.

I love you and I miss you so much.

Photo: The diamond, any diamond, paled to the beauty of my mother-in-law

ONCE FERAL, TWICE TAME

You rule with a powerful paw and
a sharp claw.
Mew, hiss, and caterwaul.
Little tiger
weighing in at just sixteen pounds

Young enough to reign for years to come.
Mature enough to wear your stud jowls
with an air of confidence.
Protect and defend your females and offspring.

Last one to take food from my hand.
Yet, the first to let me hold you.
Now, you drape your big head over my shoulder.

Giving me your trust,
while taking my heart.
Warming my soul,
while fulfilling my dream—
feral no more

WHY DID SHE HAVE TO DIE?

It's been more than ten years since my mother died. That is damn long enough.

* * *

I grew up in the second half of the twentieth century with cartoons, fairy tales, and comic books turned into animated super heroes by the entertainment industry.

Popeye the sailor man never lost a fight with Brutus; spinach was the magic bullet to keeping Olive Oyl. Tom never caught Jerry; the cat's mouth was always avoided in some lame way by the cute little mouse. Did Fred Flintstone or Wilma ever have to go on living after the death of a loved one?

Hell no!

Snow White wakes up from a long sleep, after Prince Charming kisses her. In the Three Lives of Thomasina, the cat comes back after being killed by a car. With the help of her fairy godmother, Cinderella not only goes to the ball, she gets the prince.

Superman just spins the world counter clockwise on its axis and Lois Lane is alive again. When the mild-mannered David Banner can't handle a situation, he turns into the Incredible Hulk to save the day. The Caped Crusader's alter-ego is a billionaire with a Batcave, Batmobile, a bullet proof and fire-resistant bat uniform. He uses defensive, non-lethal weapons to protect and defend Gotham City. And, he's the only character dealing with the death of someone—both parents.

Life isn't a cartoon or a fairy tale, and super heroes are only in comic books or the movies.

Intellectually, I understand death, but emotionally I want a Superwoman uniform and the first thing I would do is spin the earth counter clockwise ten years, two-hundred and fifty-five days.

"Hi, Mom."

BY A MERE SHAKE

Life isn't one-directional.
It's more like an Etch-A-Sketch drawing—
lines move up, down, side-to-side,
curve and sometimes
spiral out of control.

It takes just a movement
for the clear image
to distort or disappear.
Life can be erased by a mere shake—
whatever created
is often lost, forever.

It can never look the same.
Life will feel fleeting and unsteady,
with your foundation gone.
Can you re-build it?
No, but you can build
something different.
Where do you start?

The Etch-A-Sketch knobs
are in your hands.
From this moment on,
draw whatever you want.
It won't be the same,
but it can still be good.

Turn the knobs and start over—
that's all you can do.

This piece was modified from "Etch A Sketch."
Hinkle, Debra Davis, and Jim Leonard. Tears to Laughter:
Embracing the Future Without Forgetting the Past, Page 37.
Dac Say Publishing, 2013.

MURDER OR MANSLAUGHTER?

I want to know if it would be second degree murder or just manslaughter. It felt intentional to me. I'm getting ahead of myself; let me start at the beginning.

* * *

On July 2, 2016 I was standing outside a local pet store with a feline organization trying to find a new home for a kitten that I was fostering.

Suddenly, I smelled smoke and realized that my asthma inhaler was in my purse locked in my car. Oh shit. I'm in trouble.

I look around and locate the man smoking; he is upwind of me and very near my car. *How was I going to get to my inhaler?* I had to do the moving and if I didn't get to my inhaler fast enough to stop or even lessen the attack, I didn't want to even imagine what would happen. I moved, gasping all the way, a hundred feet or so southwest of where I had been, and sat down to rest before I tried to get my medication.

A worried bystander came up to me after I moved and asked if he could help. I couldn't talk, but I pointed to the smoker and the man seemed to understand. I probably scared that kind man.

The Good Samaritan went to talk to the smoker and I snuck back to my car to get the lifesaving medication, still gasping for air and now praying, too.

I used my inhaler several times and I was still having trouble. I could talk now, but I was clearly not breathing easily. The Good Samaritan came back and related the conversation he'd had with the smoker. "He refused to put out the cigarette and he said it was your problem. He wouldn't even move." I thanked the man for his good intentions.

I called 911 and requested that an officer come out and cite the smoker. I told the operator that I was fine. She didn't believe me because in just a few minutes the rescue squad arrived, and they weren't wearing police uniforms.

I was pissed at this point. Not only was the man smoking illegally, he wasn't even going to be ticketed for it.

Sometime, while I was on the phone the nice man came back and gave me the license plate number for the vehicle the smoker drove away in. I thanked him profusely for his effort, in between wheezes and gasps. I almost forgot, one of the other volunteers returned my kitten in his cage, before or after the fire department arrived, all five or six of them.

It's chaos at this point. I try hard to listen to the rescue guy, watch my kitten, and keep track of my phone and keys. Let me not forget the note with the license number on it. In other words, I'm overwhelmed.

* * *

You would think that San Luis Obispo County, California, where it is illegal to smoke outside, would be the ideal place for someone who is chemically sensitive to cigarette smoke. What that means is that I have an asthma attack if I encounter a few particulates (distinct particle or matter) per million of smoke residue. But how could I come across smoke because, as of May of 2010 it is illegal to smoke in all areas frequented by the public?

However, police will not actively enforce the smoking ban, but may issue citations for violations. There lies the problem. The smoker can break the law with little or no consequences, and I can end up in the emergency room. That is exactly how I ended up in the ER, all because someone had to smoke illegally, and I had a reaction to it. *Damn. Double damn.*

* * *

There isn't a lot to do when you are in a bed, listening to the noises of the machines hooked up to you in the emergency room. I found myself lost in thought about my asthma. *Why didn't the inhaler work quicker, better? How long will the symptoms, congestion and breathing problems last this time? How many more times am I going to be okay after an asthma attack? Am I going to die like my childhood friend, Debbie Cash, from lack of air due to an asthma induced episode?* The EMT and the doctor are worried about my heart, primarily. It is beating too fast.

Then I start thinking about how my clothes have been peeled off me and a semi-open backed excuse for a gown replaces them. This is after the ambulance ride to the local hospital that I was intimidated, not frightened, into taking.

I'm stuck in a bed with all these machines hooked up to me. *Beep. Beep.* This one tracks my heart via eight to ten leads glued to various parts of my anatomy. These leads replace the ones put on during the ride to the hospital. The little monitor on my right index finger tracks my pulse. *Beep. Beep.* And then the blood pressure cuff tightens almost beyond my pain tolerance. Oh, I forgot the drip with the saline solution. *Beep. Beep.*

I'm in the bed next to the doctors' and nurses' break or supply room so it seems someone is walking by every minute. The commotion is annoying, and it's especially bothering because I can't go anywhere. And now I have to go to the bathroom. I'm just a little bit grumpy and maybe slightly scared. Yeah, just a little bit grumpy. I guess I am feeling helpless and not in control. I'm angry with the smoker, too.

The technician arrives to take a chest x-ray. As soon as she begins to unwind the machine's cords, she gets a page and runs off to take an emergency x-ray. "I'll be back," she says, looking over her shoulder.

* * *

Most people are familiar with second-hand smoke—it's when you encounter the exhaled particulates of a smoker's cigarette or cigar.

A least 250 of the 7,000 chemicals in secondhand smoke are known to be harmful, i.e. ammonia, hydrogen cyanide and carbon monoxide. Almost 70 of the toxic chemicals in secondhand tobacco smoke cause cancer, including arsenic. That stat scares me. Does it scare you?

I don't think many people know what third-hand smoke is. I know I didn't, even when I have reacted to it. It is the toxic tobacco residue left clinging to something, i.e. clothes, car interior, carpet, etc. The residue is low, but it can be very harmful to human beings. My reaction to it is an asthma attack, just like to the first and second-hand smoke.

Most people have heard of, and even seen, someone having an asthma attack. But even if you are standing next to the person, you don't know exactly what they feel. You know that you are scared, and you're not sure exactly how to help them.

Multiply your fears until you feel absolute terror, and then you know what the person having the asthma attack feels during an episode.

Asthma gets progressively worse, so if you've had it for a long time or you've had many attacks, another one can be your last. That's your fear, and sometimes it's a reality.

* * *

If the smoker had only walked away, or, better yet put his cigarette out, or, best yet, obeyed the law, I wouldn't have been burdened with: (a) an ambulance ride, (b) three hours in the emergency room and, (c) almost ten thousand dollars' worth of medical bills. I'm not even counting the extreme fear, the breathing problems I have for the next few days, and the additional doctor's appointment, and medications for the sinus infection I end up with.

Where in Chapter 8.16 of the San Luis Obispo Municipal Code do I get reimbursed? Or, does the smoker pay for the damages he caused? When I die from exposure to first or second-hand smoke, is the smoker going to be charged with murder, or manslaughter?

HUSBAND

Scan QR code to listen to poem.

Picked me up
when I fell—
helped me dust the dirt off.

Held me up,
when I couldn't stand—
from grief that seized me.

Sustained me
when I faltered—
told me to try again.

Embraced me
when I was afraid—
from a nightmare or a memory.

Encouraged me
when I needed a friend—
by telling me all my good qualities.

Was painfully honest
when I needed the truth—
to move to the next echelon.

* * *

Stood long and close enough
to see me stand-alone—
accomplished.

Now we walk together,
side by side—
holding each other's hand.

I dedicated this poem to my husband, Roland, on the inside cover of my first published work in December 2005.

SECTION THREE

Shirley Radcliff Bruton

Dedication

I must begin with Firenze Crawford, my mentor, guide, and friend. Out of a genuine love for humanity and her quiet, joyful way, Firenze drew out the innate talents of others. It was within this influence that I started to share my poetry.

Richard L. Bruton (a.k.a. Dick) was kind enough to drop to one knee and ask for my hand in marriage. His hand is always there for me, embracing, touching, opening car doors, messing with the TV remotes, building me desks, cluttering the house, changing light bulbs, taking on more chores and all the gardening so I have more time to write. He's an artist/designer, good editor, and excellent poet. His encouragement has been my mainstay. Without it, I would not have approached the Friday Night Writers' Group. He laughs out loud and cries openly. He's honest and forthright with his opinions and is simply my shining star. Thanks to Richard L. Bruton for the sketches at the beginning of each of my sections.

Author's Bio

Shirley Radcliff Bruton is a poet, modern dancer, choreographer, and performance artist. She scripts, stages, and directs interdisciplinary artists and unskilled performers to convey her conceptual narratives. Shirley has worked both in California and New York City, where she lived for nine years while working for the Merce Cunningham Dance Foundation.

Bruton loves the macro lens and often uses it in her performance work. It gives her the ability to examine things up close — woven fabric, sections of the human body, insects, moss, etc. The subtleties of black and white photography can create a mysterious mood, like shadows, becoming an entrance into another realm of seeing. Her poems compile essences and desires and access the tactile to discover and observe life.

OUTSIDE

When my sisters and I got too rowdy indoors, Mom would say, "Why don't you girls go outside and play?" We spent hours outside with kids from the neighborhood and/or our imaginations.

The soft blossoms hang over
the flat splintered wooden fence
rigidly holding its watch
as it divides the landscape

On the impulse of a wind
the branches whisper their song
tiny white petals sweep
across the drawn weathered planks
over and over again

After an all too brief encounter
they sail away in clusters
lifting falling rolling
spreading out and gathering again
only to take off on the next zephyr

Tickling their own fancy jovial selves
their dance alerts us all
to the arrival of redesign
abandonment and renewal

The fence is sadly left behind defending
its territory until spring returns
to gently smooth its solitary hold

AGING WONDERS

Scan QR code to listen to poem.

Full, delicate, aging wonders
droop voluptuously
long, leggy stems barely able
to support their lust

The large, heavy roses surrender
the weight of their last hurrah
into the palms of my hands
my face caresses theirs

Petals fall, fragile, pale
layer upon silky layer slipping
away like snow blanketing the earth
with its memories

My silhouette reaches long and thin,
stretching into the stillness of the afternoon
light, edges dissolving into the continuum

LAYERS

The gentle breeze
moves cautiously through dense web
of intertwining branches, leaves shimmer
buds and blossoms rub against one another
clinging to each other like rigid, gangly arms
pulsing in unison

Rose bushes teeming in the prime of their fullness
create a canopy: the hollow below a sanctuary of
fallen petals, dried leaves, and creatures

Birds and mice and dragonflies are protected
from the racing children, who dare not venture
into the densely populated thorns

Even the bees and hummingbirds are safe
from the screams of boys and girls and shouting
adults who seem oblivious to this enchanted
patch of life filled with exotic scents and colors
that create odd stirrings from within the deepest
realms of my layered psyche

Originally published in The Tribune, San Luis Obispo in April 2011.

ROCKS

Rocks full of color in water
pale in the noon sunlight
slowly changing into dust

Spiders are quick to flee
frogs jump their plumpness
from rounded edge to rounded edge

Sleek, angular grasshoppers
maneuver the air like puppets on a string
quickly rising and landing

Look under the rocks, she advised
and I did
beneath the surface
beetles and worms, in respite
captured the dark, moist, coolness

Found any gold yet? he joked
and I did
to dream the day away
is a desire highly sought after
to discover yourself amongst rocks
is the dream come true

JUST BEYOND

A *conversation with myself*

Knee-high grasses rise up between me
and the country fence a few yards away

Just beyond that, I see a wooded area
with bushes and a clearing, and a winding path,
it draws me into its enchantment

I look about for access and see
a slightly open gate
Does that mean I'm invited?

The soft light of the setting sun beckons me
tranquil and delicate
so tempting

But the shadows, ever growing in the late afternoon,
defy my passage, I could get lost in the dark—
too daunting

Going into the unknown is the adventure
reluctance, the unwilling mate

I can imagine what's out there,
I whisper
Really, is that enough?
I'll return, I say
knowing I won't

Selected for the Discovery in Art and Poetry Exhibition,
Atascadero, CA Library
April-May 2017

AN INVITATION TO WINTER

On the wings of a fall wind
trees release the influence of spring
and their abundant canopy of summer

Parched leaves drop and toss about
in a torrent of crackling frenzy
scooting across the flight decks of driveways
parking lots and streets

The only accent to this rapid, hypnotic pace
mesmerizing in its lack of detail
is a hard thud as acorns hit the deck
like bullets shot from a tree

When it rains, a spirit of murky wetness ensues
leaves cling to each other unable to pull themselves
apart from their new-found intimacy
a soggy brew of reduction begins to rot into the earth,
becoming a fine cuisine for the worms

The cycle repeats itself again and again,
until the leaves of deciduous trees pile up,
shielding the land against the angst of winter

IMPETUOUS STORM

A heavy mist fills the air.
Drips stockpile into droplets
falling randomly
plopping, splashing.

A frog's singular call
squeaks through
the dampness.

Dark heavy clouds gather,
forming a lid over the landscape,
sealing in a portentous future.

Water begins to pour from the sky.
The downfall switches from vertical
to horizontal to sideway slants.
The attack is relentless,
demanding full surrender.

Sloshing through rising puddles
shoes fill quickly, scooping up
the moisture in unmeasured doses.

A hand-held umbrella turns inside out,
pulls away, and flies down the road,
hardly a match for the brooding storm.

The upheaval is impetuous and unpredictable.
Soaked clothes cling to bodies, the weight
and volume becomes arduous.

Without warning, the dark lid lifts,
exposing a stew of mud, fallen branches,
and submerged pathways, lying next to rivulets
of water escaping into storm drains.

As the ominous clouds begin to pull apart,
white, puffy, whip-cream shapes
glide across the sky. The sun radiates around
the edges obsessively bright and brilliant,
hustling in the drama of its return.

Meanwhile, wet, shiny and unastonished
in the midst of pools of water
a familiar croaking is heard.

A measured serenade sings into the soggy calm.
The anuran lays claim to his territory,
and begs the company of another.

THE OLD OAK TREE

The old oak tree rises up through the opening
    created for it on our front deck
        its hollow center fills with leaves
    rainwater and trapped insects, a murky
smelly, gooey, substance grows

We try to remove the caldron with thick gloves
    but the infusion of adversity coats the
        edges, the buildup becomes a viscous
    black resin, protecting it as the opening
deepens and widens each year

Big, thick, gnarly limbs rise up
    twisting and turning
        reaching, dipping and climbing again
    deep rivulets mark them
etched pathways for the rain

A fine green moss spreads its softness around
    the coarse surface, Spanish lichen gather in
        clusters, the delicacy dangles,
    teasing the deer with its stylish flare
a fallen branch provides the treat they enjoy

Nickolaus loves to run up the branches,
   clutching the rough bark, hovering like a wild
      cat; birds flit about pecking at things,
   gathering resources, stashing food or
looking about for more lucrative gains

Wild jungle sounds emanate from squirrels
   during their frenetic dances with each other,
      fluffy tails twitching, they scale the trunk;
   spiders quietly elaborate their webs,
enticing the innocence of insects

 Hidden, just beneath the moss, in the crack
   and crevices of the bark, an intricate
      arrangement of life exists, balanced,
   purposeful, edifying; perhaps the tree's
salient nature enjoys these offerings

Does it stand a little taller
   and reach a little wider each year,
      recognizing its own prominence, its own
   usefulness? It will probably outlive me
I certainly hope so

CRYSTALS

Scan QR code to listen to poem.

The cold, cold air
keeps the sun's warmth at bay
by mid-morning the frost
still coats everything

Layer upon layer of crystals
cling to each other
splaying across windows
lingering on tops of cars
collecting their intercourse
into a thin crusted glaze
of frozen seduction

Their binding stillness eventually
dissolves into the persistent sunlight
like sandcastles at the beach
surrendering their complex beauty
to the incoming tides

THE WHITE DUST OF WINTER

Looking out on the frigid morning
I see the white dust of winter
blanketing everything

Sequestered indoors, my hands, parched
and rough wrap around a cup of coffee
the hot liquid reaches down into my belly
with its warmth

At times I hear dry branches falling off trees
some hang limp before dropping to the ground
others pull away with a loud crack

Circling inside myself, the day's activities
seem like pieces of a puzzle lying around
waiting for me to assemble them
into a complete picture of a day on hold

JEO'S GARDEN

It's hidden, but not
the growth reaches out
beyond and above the fence

To find the gate
turn right on a dead-end street
right again at the graveled
entranceway and park

How many hours a day
do you spend in your garden, I ask,
As many as I can, Jeo replies
smiling with the complexities
of a face that shows deep satisfaction
delight and curiosity, all at the same time

Sunflowers tower into the tops of fruit trees
hungry for the light, their faces move
throughout the day
sweet peas cling to fencing, their scents
perfuming the air
luscious roses stand tall, deep inhalations
remind me of childhood yards

Figs cluster together, gathering
in deep purples, or greens
tomatoes hang their red bellies from vines
rows of corn and string beans, hot peppers
and salad delights nestle into beds
low lying squash ramble about freely
there's more, so much more and
it all wants to excel

Muse and investigator
study the controlled chaos
questions join together with samples
of fresh fruit and veggies
beer, wine or martinis are often added
no pairing is needed

Gardens are for working and harvesting, this one
includes sitting at makeshift tables, visiting under
umbrellas in weathered chairs and the opportunity
to step onto well-walked pathways

Containers circle the garden like guardians
holding the overspill of garlic, onions
and everything else that doesn't fit

A bench by the chicken coop, offers a place
to sit and listen to the chatter and banter
of hens while imitating their sounds

Jeo's focus and intent matches the breezes
that come through, touching everything
including me

PORTRAITS

These word pictures create a dramatic or whimsical rendering of real or imagined people.

THE BURDEN OF SUFFERING

Watching her I imagined
ancient coins dangling
from her gaunt, drawn face

Like ritualistic reminders
of servitude
and past sacrifices

Without gesturing
or flinching
she elicits pathos

The burden of suffering
is upon her and all those who
come into contact with her

THE LAST PARTY

Perhaps it was all the well-designed parties
that left her staring into herself
seated, unable to move

Clear crystal glassware
teacups, saucers, platters
vases and tiny plates
rested on a pale blue tablecloth
colorless reminders
that something was about to happen

Her hat, almost too big
for her delicate features
drooped over the top of her head
like a partially deflated balloon

An almost lifeless
internal ticking
held her in a trance

Until she moved
to lock the front door
and blow out the candles

THE MILESTONE

I met his loving affectionate eyes first
he came into full view later
revealing his kind, sensitive nature

From the jump he never took his eyes off her
the dancer I ran, leaped, turned and
twisted into lyricism with, he now holds,
embraces, sways and undulates with

A partnership developed
and like a sumi-e brush painting
rough moments became smoother
narrow edges widened
tonal differences barely noticeable
feathering off into delicate songs of gentleness

He also captured the heart of her mother
until her life ended; Rolande's beautiful light
touched his and they journeyed together
she flirted, he smiled

His friendship with my husband
as though kindred spirits
reunited after a brief absence

And now he turns 65 –
the milestone to celebrate
is how lucky we all are
to be in this life with this man

SWEPT INTO THE DEPTHS OF HUMILITY

Exhausted, she sits back on her bed
sighing, moaning, no longer curious

Her breasts hang loosely, as her arthritic hands
reach down to stroke her gnarly feet and
swollen ankles

Accepting defeat, she's swept into the depths
of humility and sinks into her final slumber

PARCHED LIPS

Tight, rigid, resentful lips remain closed
parched and cracked like the desert floor

The loose skin around her left eye pulls
upward, drawing attention to her critique

Downcast lines permanently etch her face
further enhancing the appearance
of displeasure

Her inability to verbalize
leaves one to wonder, or not
as to her sizzle

SHE WALKED INTO THE ROOM

She walked into the dimly lit room
saltine crackers covered the floor

Fire shot out from the side walls
darting in and out like a lizard's tongue
hot time tonight

Without hesitation she stepped on the crackers
crossing over to the other side
monkeys were dancing on the table tops
giraffes and elephants talking at the bar
and bunnies scurried about on the floor

She felt oddly out of place and was wondering
who recommended this place to her and why
she was definitely overdressed

As she approached the ladies room
things quieted down
to a dull whisper

Inside, perched upon a big fluffy pillow
a leopard greeted her
recumbent, submissive, alluring
tilting its head slightly to the left
and lifting its chin, as though wanting
a scratch, or a rub; she decided to leave

On her way out, she easily glided back
over the crushed crackers
soft shoeing it without lifting her feet
an easy turn and she was facing the party

She blew everyone a kiss
bowed, and left

TAWANA

My daughter Tawana
    arrived circuitously
        shyly entering my life
           at the age of eight
She was hungry for a mom
    and eager to be a child
        I found out, I was eager to be a mom
           hungry for my child
With her, deep, richly dark
    beautiful eyes
      and a trusting innocence
         I fell in love with her
We crossed over into a family
    and lived tumultuously
        in the anarchy of her dad's confusion
          for the next six years
Demanding a bond of love
    our needs and affections were deeper
        than we could have imagined
         she of me, I of her

The commitment
      at times an obligation
            not easy
                  for either of us
An elemental link
      propelled us down the streets
            of Hoboken, Manhattan
                  Binghamton and beyond
We struggled over the years
      appearing, disappearing
            reappearing like the seasons
                  reseeding our love, our pact
I like to think of our ancestors
      as a lineage stretching over
            continents, biases
            cultures
  An amalgamation of earthly planets
      African and European, aligning themselves
            so that we keep our
                  interstellar appointments
On the eve of her thirty-eighth year
      I realize we've been looking out
            for one-another
                  nearly three decades
Mothers are ever present
      whether they birth you or not
            I'm happy to be in the fold
                  of profound fulfillment

DICK

If you're over sixty-five, the nickname Dick is often used for Richard. Not so with the younger generation. My husband wears the name proudly, no pun intended. When we were first dating, I often thought to myself, there's something about Dick — and there is. These are some of my love poems.

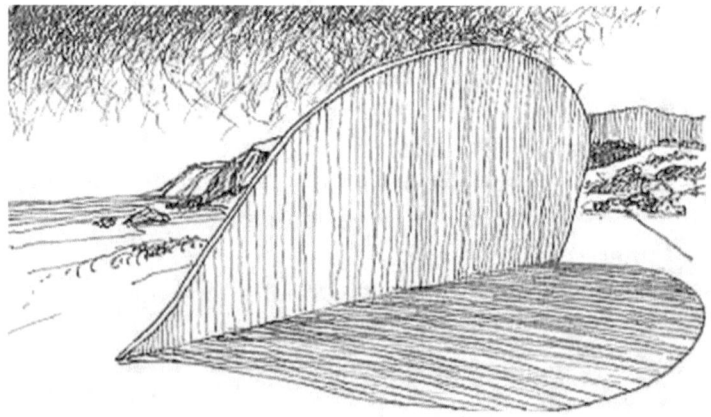

FOCUS

Our lives, important to get
to know one another first
focus I say to myself, focus
so you don't have to keep asking
him the same questions

A fantasy ripens
bodies swathe, sweet, sweet lips meld
heart to beating heart

Help me get beyond my desires
I whisper and then ask
myself – Why, is it too soon?

You, you, you and my
uncontainable overflow
What did he say?

THE JOURNEY BEGINS

The second time was brighter
it's nice to watch the ease
with which he moves through life

I breathe in his kindness
and imagine our bodies
gently touching

It's too early I say
it's too early
to make love to him

But I can sense a gentle mist
against my skin and see
the passion of our affections

To contain my feelings
is to control the current
of moving waters

We are not yet known in the future
but we sing songs of our past
joyfully for one another

Ever watchful of the experiences
yet to come, we witness a complex mystery
unfolding like a butterfly to a flower

We drift into the depths of each other
a little more each day
as the journey begins

ABOUT LOVE

Coarse, fibrous wings
landed on my door step

They mingled with mine
and we left them there

We discovered new,
softer feathers

They covered us and lifted us
into the migration of the heart

BEWITCHED

Warm, wet, sticky, yummy
fluid, merging
energizing

Bristly facial hair, broad square jaw
beautiful wide smile
sweet ass, great thighs
inquiring, searching eyes

What I whisper
knowing there is no answer
only a deeper sense of one another

Wrapping myself around
his willingness, his generosity
what a joy to be explored by his hands
to dance rhythmically with his body

The more we give, the more intense
is our pleasure of one another
freeing us to surrender to our passion

Goodness gracious...
my, my, my

NOONTIME FANTASIES

Walking among the roses today
I'm reminded of the gazebo that
sheltered our love, our secret.

In the heat of the noonday sun,
scented roses formed a laced arbor
draping and tenting us from the
rest of the world. Intimacy was ours.

Our tenderness was playful, and we
were seduced by it. Sunlight and shadows
made their way across us, a duet of rhythms
We came to know our desires, as we
folded into one another. The promise
of future delights became enticing.

There were times when we hardly
moved. Was it hesitation or intoxication?
We seemed to fly lazily around each
other like bees laden with sweet pollen.

It clung to us, as we wandered back
to work. Soft and gooey in thought,
intent and desire.

THE MORNING LIGHT

The morning light struggles
to come into my bedroom
but darkness surrounds me
like a heavy fog.

Wanting your searching hands
to cross over my body, I lie numb,
sinking back into a deep, deep, sleep.
Lost in my dreams. Thank God
I'm lost in my dreams.

Banjo Eyes cuddles and his sweetness
slowly pulls me up out of the mire
to pet his soft fur. I tell him how much
I miss you. Tears burn across my eyes,
trying to find a way out.

You've renamed my cats, my life, and now
you're gone.

4 U

My love 4U is boundless
you wrote on a post-it

With one quick stroke of the pen
a heart surrounded the 4 and U
boundless was underlined
to emphasize measurement
or, lack thereof

When the glue wore out
scotch tape held the reminder
of your love, above my kitchen sink
reassuring me during those insecure
days/weeks/months that I lived
like a single woman
waiting — waiting — waiting
to join you again

OUR BREATH

When you said there was nothing
I could do that would ever make
you leave, I was lifted, released
into the vast unknown regions
of us.

I welcome the angels, who
do not fear the demons; those
unexpected visitors rising and
falling with as much ease as an
inhale and exhale.

The breath only knows its own rhythm.
It's full sometimes and shallow others.
It doesn't ask why we explore one another,
go a little deeper, or farther, it just responds.

EVERYTHING'S OKAY

It's hot, very hot and dry
spider webs drape across
the deck's railing, capturing
light, dust, leaves and insects

The intricate, raddled silk, rises
and falls on the shallow breath
of the afternoon

In this quiet moment, I know
your warm inviting kisses
full and luxurious and your scent
part musk, mulch and sweet patchouli

Everything's okay
I just miss you

STEPPING INTO AND OUT OF DARKNESS

It was dark
I was alone
he left me a few minutes ago

My heart constricted
tight as a drawn bow
the arrow long
piercing
on target

Why now after all these years
after all the declarations of love
I asked myself

He couldn't keep her waiting
but was willing
to leave me

I could drive somewhere
I thought
stay somewhere else
tonight or longer

I walked softly
into the dark night
and the dream ended

      * * *

We were staying with family
he came to bed shortly after dawn
I think it was the alcohol
on his breath
that prompted my deeply upsetting dream

It disturbed me for hours
until he embraced me
his love
held me close
his kindness
enabled me to step back
into reality

YOUR DREAMS, MY TATTOO, OUR DRUMBEAT

Scan QR code to listen to poem.

What are your dreams made of
     my sweet husband?
     Slumber will claim you
     from me one day
     or me from you.
     Sadness grows within
     this passing thought.

Your imprint forever embossed,
     a silken stain, feathering
     its way across my body
     seeping into my pores
     like a tattoo.

A drum beat of us, always
     in my heart.

OTHER

Other captures an assortment of different experiences.

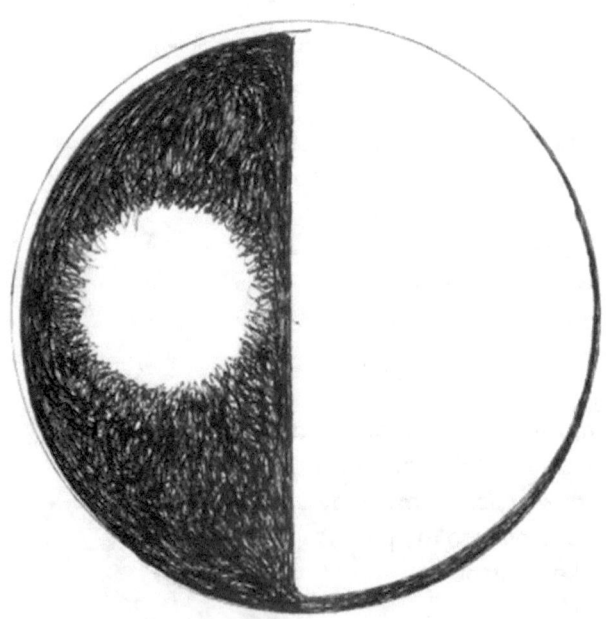

THE SLIDING GLASS DOOR

Albi, always upbeat and happy to see me, and I him, my good friend and masseur. The walk to his massage room is a series of pathways — pavers, wooden steps, chimes, statuaries and plants — arm in arm with nature. At the sliding glass door, surrender washes over me like a warm mist, its vapors urging me to leave my sandals, all responsibilities and goals behind.

* * *

Inhaling the calmness of his room
my body and mind
sigh with relief

Shedding the outer layer of me
I yield to his expert generosity
of purpose

Albi never speaks
unless to ask me to move
a little to the right or left, or roll over

The massage is deep and penetrating
offering daydreams, fragments
of thoughts, and sleep

Different parts of my body render
insights into the past, present and future
without judgement

As the hour and half comes to a close
I feel the warm energy of his hands
through the blanket, moving in a circular
motion on my belly

He pauses, then moves one hand
to my upper chest, pauses again
and then to the crown of my head

I say to myself
I'll pay attention this time and sense exactly
when he lifts both hands

But he waits for my energy to stabilize
once again, I'm lost in the fine tuning
I hear the sliding glass door open and close
he's gone; I'm in stillness

* * *

Feeling like a sea sponge
full of pores and channels
water and oxygen circulating everywhere
I try to stretch

I float in heaviness
attached to the ocean's floor
with no desire to rise

As a boneless, saturated human sponge
pulling myself up from the table
is a huge effort

My clothes don't feel the same
I whisper, what is this outer garment covering?
I'm no longer in that body

* * *

It's my turn to open and close the sliding
glass door
Are those my sandals? Is that
impression mine?
I hesitate
Am I stepping back into obligations,
destinations and concerns?

I begin the long walk back to Albi's porch
my legs don't move quite like they did before

Gravity seems to draw my feet down, deep
into the earth, each step lifts sod and roots
attached to the uncoiling fern
living inside me

One of his cats, lounging about, pulls me
into familiar territory and I find the right trail
Albi and I embrace and I tell him about his
special gift

Distracted by the soft afternoon light, deer
on the hillside, the ease with which
he speaks I slowly move back into who I
think I am

The effects of my monthly massage, like the lunar cycle, slowly wane. At the last phase of the crescent shape, I'm held, rocked and lifted day by day towards the waxing fullness waiting for me at the sliding glass door

FILIGREE

Passing over me without lingering
ephemeral patterns filter through
the branches of old oaks and pines

I watch my own shadow-hand
reach out across plants and rocks

In a filigree of subtlety I whisper
my name over and over looking
for an imprint of myself

As darkness begins its drape,
the moon, constellations and
shooting stars will light the way
for nocturnal spirits

But for those of us who use daylight
as an usher, we wait until the morning
returns to once again search for ourselves
in contrasting shapes of light and dark

MY SCENT

The cloth billows out
its fine woven pattern
imprinted with words and drawings

A mysterious language
appearing and disappearing
between the crafted folds

Expressions
seem to collect themselves
with an almost
not there
button

Light captures it
folds darken it
like a shawl opening and closing in a dance
suspended in the movement
a rapture of subtlety

I wrap myself in its magic
and can feel it around my shoulders
brushing against my bare arms
dusting off my scent like pollen

It becomes airborne
in dust particles
that sparkle in light
and dim in the shade
landing on others and inhaled
into the recesses of their desires

All because of a cloth
a mysterious language
and a button holding it all together

SLUMBERING RAIN CLOUDS

We walked around the parched, cracked lake
the air was thick and cool
rain clouds slumbered
across the sky
teasing us

It felt tropical and I was transported to a softer
side of myself, like feeling the spray
from a waterfall barely
reaching my skin
it's inviting
elating

Not even a bead of water fell on us that morning
later, a cloud, stretching aimlessly, woke up
releasing a few large drops
over our deck
some even
touched
me

ASH

The wind blows the fire quickly
through the canyons and hillsides
its scorching hands reach deep and wide

Smoke billows
spreading its pallid
brown stains across the sky

Ash rains down, dry, lifeless
coating everything with the burnt remains
of homes, everything inside, trees
grasses, insects, frogs, fleeing birds
deer caught up in the fast moving flames
cats, dogs, horses, and other pets
left behind in a quick evacuation

We inhale the residue of it all
there doesn't seem to be an exhale
it's irritating, congesting, bothersome
life threatening to asthmatics

Crazy drought, giving way to fires of hunger
beyond reason, burning without passion
the loss is sad, painful, some weep openly
will the birds sing again
sure, we say *of course they will*

* * *

The flames and ash of wars also surround us
they're not as obvious as the waves of brown
clouds or the white dust on our cars

They're directed by another kind of wind
the kind that surges
from the human breath
of greed and bigotry

Are those fleeing their countries
unlike those of us
forced to leave our homes
by a fast-moving fire
beyond our control

Do we not inhale the ashes of entrapment
executions and destructions of towns
villages and people

We head for shelters
others head for refugee camps
how much does a family in need, need
can they rebuild and sing again
with uncertainty, we say
we hope so

A GATHERING

My two sisters and one special cousin come together
once a year for four days. At first it was tents and campfires,
now it's vacation homes with fireplaces. It's been ongoing
for over twenty years.

Our arms wrap around each other and
I'm surrounded in the familiar warmth
of the women in my family
their presence soft, welcoming,
imparts only a fraction of the
intimacy we hold for one another.

A yearly gathering, a gift, a respite
we leave politics, religion, and current
events behind and accept each other
as is, there are better stories to tell,
celebrations to sing, losses to lament
tears to share.

Around a fire, the self-melts
in a hot cleanse of crackling wood
red, blue and yellow designs
change into gray dust by dawn

as the evening passes, we slowly
conjure up our deepest considerations
some we share, some we don't.

We have walked softly in a forest
admiring a mother bear and her cubs
while keeping a watchful eye out
for our own innocence

stood quietly, in intimacy
away from human sounds
and saw an owl, also in silence,
swoop down from behind us,
into the tall pines and redwoods
with power and determination

praised delicate wild flowers
at a trail's edge; their petals
seem to open wider and their
colors deepen as we passed

It's a rare gathering, our special circle
uninterrupted with twists and turns
like a Moebius Band, challenging
our orientation

inclusive to us, but drawing in others
as we speak of them.

Deepening our bond every passing year
with decades of growing up, growing older
and heading into the elder years

we witness the aging process and our
place in it, knowing the day will come
when we are three, then two, then one
and none.

While that's sad to consider
it's of no real consequence
for the melodies we've created
and the footprints left behind
will remain forever an imprint
on the fabric of life

I would be envious, if I weren't
already a part of it.

SECTION FOUR

Susan Tuttle

Dedication

I dedicate these stories to my son, Aaron Kondziela, whose support and belief in me has been the lynchpin of my life. His can-do attitude toward everything has helped me reevaluate the way I approach life.

His talent with computers, music and graphic design, and his caring for and willingness to help others, leave me speechless in awe. I rest more secure at night (when I'm not up writing, killing people on paper) knowing he is in the world.

Maybe he'll even read one or two of these stories... I did use a computer to do the layouts!

Author's Bio

Susan Tuttle is the slightly twisted author of three suspense novels, an indieB.R.A.G. Medallion-awarded paranormal suspense novel, a literary historical suspense novel, and a collection of award-winning short stories. She is also a professional freelance editor and writing instructor/mentor. Her comprehensive 6-volume *Write It Right: Exercises to Unlock the Writer in Everyone* workbook series is based on her writing classes, for fiction writers of all levels.

Susan is past president of SLO NightWriters and the Central Coast Chapter of Sisters in Crime, and is presently the newsletter editor for both organizations. Her work has garnered numerous awards in various writing competitions and has appeared in Mind Prints Literary Journal, Tolosa Press, If & When Literary Journal, The Feathered Flounder Literary Journal and in anthologies from SLO NightWriters and Central Coast SinC.

A native of Buffalo, New York, Susan moved to California in 2004. She now lives on the Central Coast of California with her imaginary cat in a house filled with her (mostly unfinished) handmade quilts and (mostly finished) knitted scarves.   She is presently at work on a new mystery series featuring her female P.I., Skylark, who has paranormal abilities, and two young adult (YA) fantasy series.

THE CONFESSION

Bless me, Father, for I have sinned. Can't remember last time I did this; I was probably about 12, whatever age I was when I got confirmed. No one ever asked me if I wanted to do it; I just went along with the program. Given my Pa and those nuns, it was easier that way. Kinda like the way my whole life has gone so far.

It probably all started because of my name. I've always wondered why parents don't stop to think before they saddle their kids with some of the names they come up with. Mine sure as hell didn't—if you'll excuse the French, Father. People, I've found, are basically idiots. Most of them can't think past the tip of their noses, or would know what was going on if they did. Still trying to figure out why God was so all-fired excited to create us in the first place. You ask me, He just wasted His time.

But back to the name thing. You don't give a guy a sex name and expect him to turn out like a normal man. Right? I mean, once those hormones kicked in, I had a prophesy to fulfill. What? Oh, you ready for a laugh? It's Randy. I ask you. Where were their heads when they came up with that moniker? Randy Randy they called me in high school—well, starting in 8th grade because I lost a year due to scarlet fever and had to repeat—and though it pissed me off real good, I sure was happy to make it the truth. Still am, as a matter of fact. Women get a kick out of the—what do they call it? Oh, yeah—double entendre when I introduce myself. Let me tell you, I've been in some very interesting beds over the years. Raise the hair on your nape if I started naming names. Sally Mae, now, that woman was double jointed, if you get my drift… But, seeing as you're a man of the cloth and all, maybe some things are better left unsaid.

No, that's not what I'm confessing. Hell, nothing wrong with a good roll in the hay, is there? I mean, God made us that way, preservation of the species and all, right? Can't be wrong if God made it that way. Huh? Well, sure, lots of them were married, what's that got to do with anything? You really expect someone named Randy is gonna say no when something in a skirt gives him a come-hither look? Get real, Father.

What I came in to talk about ain't the sex. That's the good part of my life. It's my second job. Don't know why, but for some reason it's starting to bother me. Never did before. But this last case…

You wouldn't think to look at me that I could be who I am. I think that's one reason the girls go crazy for me. I ain't good looking, ain't tall, don't have mesmerizing eyes or a booming voice, don't have any commanding presence. Heads don't turn when I walk into a room. I'm just an ordinary guy no one really notices. Not until I turn on the charm for the ladies, I tell you, I really got that part down. But mostly I just disappear into the woodwork, you know? I'm an accountant in the daytime. Facts, figures—no pun intended there, Father, I mean numbers not girls' bodies— shit, I even use a pocket protector and wear horn rim glasses. I'm like a stereotype, you know? So killing is the last thing you'd think when you look at me.

Yeah, I said killing. That's my second job, I do it at night. Pays real good, and me being unremarkable is a distinct advantage. Not even cops notice me, not that I stick around long after icing someone, though I could, you know? Never had a problem with it before, you know? Most of these schmucks deserve what they get.

But when they asked me to kill a woman, it kinda got to me. I'd rather stick it to her, if you know what I mean, than stick it to her. Right? I mean, yeah, there are women out there who are real bitches, who deserve to be taken out as much as the guys I rub out. But there's something about doing a woman... and Marisal, she has these big green eyes and the reddest lips you ever saw. And tits... man, they enter a room a good two minutes before she does. I ask you, is it right to eliminate that from the gene pool? No, I mean it. I need an answer. It is right? I know she slept around on Bendigo and he's really pissed, but that's what women do, right? They were made to lie on their backs and spread their legs. Why should she die for it?

But then, if she don't I won't get paid and I do have expenses. Gotta pay the berth fee for my boat, it's due next week. That fucker just keeps going up, year after year. And then there's rent, and my car payment, and... It'll be sad if Marisal is gone, but there's always another piece of ass around the next corner, right?

So, I guess that's it, then. Thanks, Father, for helping me make up my mind. Though I think I'll sleep with Marisal one last time before I off her. Or maybe twice. Bendigo's paying a lot... might as well make sure he gets his money's worth. So, I'll see you around, Father. Maybe next time I come in I really will be sorry.

NIGHT STALK

Pretty little scarf, so delicate, so dangerous. A pattern whose colors fade in and out through shades of aqua, from almost-white to dark undersea depths. Ridges and smooth places along its length; someone had taken great care in its design, its construction. Love and caring went into that long, slender snake of attire.

I watched the ends float as she walked down the street ahead of me, unaware that I followed behind. They wafted on the wind, bobbed with each movement of her lithe, curvaceous body. I knew if I held it in my hand, that scarf, I could see my own flesh and bone through its delicate weave. Though light penetrated its spaces to its inner core, still the scarf held its darkness close, a darkness that spoke to me. Did anyone else see it? Hear it?

No.

It spoke only to me, the darkness in that beauty: *Come to me, hold me, play with me. Feel me. Make me yours.* And I walked on, my steps in rhythm with her footsteps, my breath in syncopation with hers, as my hands itched, and my breath quickened. Mine, mine, mine, mine: each step another syllable in the chant, each block one more moment closer to the time.

The time of taking.

We turned into an alley, our breath white wisps in the cold night, and left all other life behind. I felt the power surge in me, felt the urgency rise, heard the scarf cry out for my hand. And so I took her, took her down in that dark alley, down onto the filth of the pavement, the obscurity of the darkness, and gave the power its freedom. I grasped that scarf, let its softness caress my fingers, watched my hands vanish into its folds, and pulled.

Yarn stretches.

Yarn binds.

Yarn owns.

And I prevailed.

In the end I took the scarf with me and left her carcass behind. Took the scarf to study, to smell, to enjoy. By myself. For myself.

I love winter cold, winter darkness. Scarf weather. They're everywhere, pretty little scarves, so delicate, so dangerous.

I'll go find another one tomorrow night.

THE ONE
A YA Fantasy Novel in Progress.

Volume 1 of the Quadrilogy

Chapter I

Destany's Daughter

The moment Meleia saw him at the top of the garden she knew her mother had died. Meleia's heart constricted in her chest and for an instant she grew lightheaded from the pain of her loss.

"No! Mamma!"

The protest escaped her lips before she could catch herself. But Meleia doubted he had heard it. It had been caught in her throat, a sound softer than the agitated bees buzzing around the fragrant hyacinth and geraniums she and her mother had planted together. Not even his ears could be that sharp.

He sat atop a huge gray stallion, his black cape lifting on the breeze. He looked like an ominous hovering raven silhouetted against the pristine clouds. He studied the garden, a careful, slow sweep of his eyes that hadn't yet reached where she sat on a bench beside a bed of roses, half-hidden by a magnolia. Meleia wondered if he would see her, recognize her for who and what she was despite a dress that blended her into the garden's riot of color—her mother's insistence on camouflage. "For when the time comes..." she'd always said, the fear in her voice making Meleia shudder. Fear that now hit Meleia with stunning force, because the time had come. And she was unprepared. And alone.

But she knew who he was, who he had to be. She lowered her head and glanced to her left. The back gate stood thirty yards away, closed and locked as usual. She fingered the key in her pocket. Could she reach the gate, open it and vanish through before he caught her? He'd not be able to travel far in this dimension, not if he was as limited as Mamma had been. But she wasn't limited because her father had come from this dimension. That gave her a chance. She slowly pulled the gate key from her pocket.

The horse whinnied. Meleia's head snapped up and she found herself looking into the man' eyes, their cold inhumanness clear even at this distance. He looked just as her mother had described him and Meleia gasped. Her heart began to pound. She leapt from the bench and raced for the gate. Stones and twigs jabbed into her bare feet, but she ignored the pain, had to ignore the pain. The horse's thundering hooves echoed loud behind her. She had the key ready in one hand and the other on the latch when he caught her. He twisted his fingers tight in her hair and yanked her up, away from freedom. She screamed and raked his hand with the key. He cried out and his fingers spasmed, then let go of her.

Meleia spun and fled in the opposite direction. He shouted her name and again she heard the horse bearing down on her. She tried to swerve, but the old willow blocked her path. He grabbed her around the waist as he raced past and lifted her into the saddle in front of him. She swung the key at him again, but he caught her wrist and wrenched it from her grasp.

"Mamma!" she shrieked, though she knew her mother could no longer hear her.

His hand closed on her neck, his thumb and forefinger digging into her chin, and pulled her head back against his chest. She clawed at his hand, his wrist, barely able to breathe, but her nails seemed to make no impact on his strength. Her vision began to blur.

She felt the horse falter when they reached the top of the garden and neared the place where the bougainvillea screened what looked to be a garden shed. Hope flared in her heart. But the man forced his will on the steed. They leapt through the scarlet blooms, through the image of the shed, and into to the dimensional portal. Electric shocks skittered through Meleia's body. Lights flashed, blinding her. Wind roared in her ears. She twisted in his grasp until her consciousness fled. The last thing she heard was her captor's triumphant laugh.

* * *

Meleia woke to deafening silence, a quiet so deep she could almost hear her own heartbeat. It felt as though years had passed since she last took a breath, and she pulled air into her lungs with an audible gasp. Her skin felt hot and tender, the way it had the time she'd been scalded by spilled boiling water. She tried to move but her watery bones defeated her. It seemed to take hours just to open her eyes.

There was no ceiling. She blinked, startled, and looked to her left, her right. No walls, just a floor that ended in abrupt darkness. And a hard, uneven surface beneath her. Where was she?

She forced herself to move. The surface she was on crinkled as she rolled to the edge and dropped down onto her feet. Memories shifted as she stood shaking, waiting for strength to return. Images kaleidoscoped before her mind's eye: the garden, the man on the horse, the portal.

Mamma!

She pressed a hand to her mouth to keep her cry from spilling out. A tear broke free and tracked down her cheek. She rubbed it away with the back of her hand. She felt broken inside, like glass crushed into tiny shards, but she couldn't afford to cry now. She had to be strong. She had to fight. She'd cry for her mother after she got away from him. Once she got home and put the garden so far behind her he couldn't follow her, could never find her again. If she could locate the portal and figure out how to activate it.

Meleia straightened her spine and looked around the room. She stood beside a crude, narrow bed with head- and footboards hacked from a dark, splintery wood. The frame balanced on four blocky legs that held it high off the floor. It held a lumpy mattress covered by a filthy, threadbare sheet through which pieces of coarse straw had poked and scratched her. A moth-eaten blanket lay crumpled at one end. No pillow. The floor, which looked like oak but felt way too cold and slick to her bare feet to be wood, was circular in shape. From where walls should have been she saw faint glimmers of light, as if there were an almost invisible barrier. She saw nothing other than the bed in the room—if one could call a place with no walls a room. No table or chair, no dresser, not even a rug on the floor. No indication of any door or window. In the darkness beyond the room she saw dim half-globes of light suspended in the air, some close, others far away, but could see no movement within or around them. No sign of anyone, anywhere.

Get out of here. Now! she told herself.

She looked around again but still found no sign of a doorway. Well, there has to be one. He put you in here, there must be a way out. She thought a moment then decided that if she couldn't see the door, perhaps she could feel it. She took a few steps over to where the floor ended and reached out to the darkness. Shocks arrowed up her arm. Sparks flew, stinging into her flesh. She yelped and jerked back. Lights still arced where she had touched the invisible wall. She stood gasping and watched them slowly fade into nothing. Then she reached out again, carefully this time, until she just touched the force field. In the light from the shooting sparks she caught a glimpse of a deep chasm beyond the place where the floor ended.

"Guess that's why they don't need walls," she muttered, rubbing a singed spot on her hand.

"Ah. You're awake," a deep male voice said. "Good."

Meleia spun. Her captor stood across the room, less than twelve feet away, legs spread wide, hands clasped behind his back, so tall she didn't think her head would come up to his shoulder. He wore all black—a silk shirt that molded to his muscular chest, leather pants that hugged his legs, metal-tipped boots on his feet. A tongue of fire seemed to smolder in the cold inhumanness of his black eyes, a flame that vanished when Meleia shook her head and blinked. He dropped his gaze down the length of her body and his thin lips lifted in a half smile. The victor inspecting his prize. A burning core of venom rose within her. Had she a weapon to hand she'd have killed him where he stood.

"Let me introduce myself," he purred.

Meleia lifted her chin and glared at him.

"Don't bother. I know who you are. Uncle."

"I see." He took a step forward and crossed his arms, seeming unaffected by the loathing in her tone. Behind him, to his right, gaped the doorway through which he'd entered the room. Meleia forced herself not to look at it and edged a step to her left. "And did your mother also tell you why you are important? Did she mention the Imperium?"

His questions confused her. Meleia frowned and bit her lip. She had no idea what he was talking about.

"I didn't think so." Her uncle's mouth again moved into a half smile. "Always the crafty one, my sister."

"She's dead. You killed her!" Meleia spat.

"Not true, niece. Destany is dead because she was willful and headstrong. Because she made stupid choices. And because she was a traitor."

Meleia's heart lurched in her chest. Her vision misted red.

"She was the bravest woman I know!"

Meleia lifted a fist, ready to strike at him. He chuckled.

"Insolent little half-breed, aren't you? You look just like her, you know, when she was sixteen. You have her smart mouth, too. I'm hoping I'll have to hurt you to get what I need."

The flame kindled again in his eyes and Meleia's breath caught in her throat. I'm not dreaming, that's real fire!

She stared, mesmerized. Then he took two paces forward, jerking her back to the present. She edged further to her left, hoping he would not realize why. He was in arm's reach of her now, and that terrified her. But every sidestep brought her closer to the gap through which he'd entered the chamber, beyond which she could see stairs descending into the dark abyss. The way out, one that hadn't been there before. She shook her head and glared at him.

"I don't care what you do. Whatever you want, you won't get it. Not from me."

"Of course, I will, niece." He raised his brows and looked over at the bed. "It's just a matter of time."

Meleia slammed her hands into his chest, shoved him sideways and raced for the doorway. Her unshod feet slipped a bit on the slick floor and her heart thudded hard enough to break through her chest wall. She ran as though the hounds of hell were at her heels, for in her mind her uncle was the personification of hell itself.

She'd leapt through the doorway and down three steps before a hard hand closed on her arm and yanked her back. She screamed as her feet skidded out from under her, a shriek that changed to a guttural groan when she cracked her ribs on a stair edge. Then her uncle swung her up and threw her back into the prison chamber. She hit the floor hard. Her breath whooshed out and her vision dimmed. Before she could scramble to her feet he jerked her upright and smacked the back of his hand into her face. Her knees buckled. She tasted blood in her mouth. He hit her again. Black spots swam before her eyes. Something warm ran from her nose.

"This is what defiance will get you, Meleia!" he shouted, shaking her until she thought her neck would snap. "How much pain do you think you can take before you give me what I need?"

Then he dropped her, spun on his heel and stalked out of the chamber. The entryway vanished, leaving Meleia alone, curled on the floor, clinging desperately to one faint trace of consciousness.

Chapter II

Meleia lay near the head of the bed, shuddering, hands pressed to her aching face. Sobs tore from within her. She hated to cry but she couldn't help it. She'd never hurt so much before, not even when she'd smiled at Jason McGregor and his girlfriend had shoved her and she'd fallen down the steps at school. Sharp stabs shot through her ribs with every breath and she couldn't stop shaking. She kept seeing the contempt in her uncle's cold eyes, the tiny fire— a real flame!—that had kindled in them when he spoke of hurting her. Do not let him near you. There's nothing in him but darkness, her mother had told her. Now Meleia understood what she'd meant.

She reached up and pulled the tattered blanket off the bed, let it spill over her quaking body. Warmth began to seep into her and the tears slowed. She lay still, blinking her eyes clear as the pain began to fade, and her head cleared. She thought about what her uncle had said—that she was important to him.

He wants something from me. What is it? And what is the Imperium? Why didn't you tell me more, Mamma? Why did you think I was too young?

All she knew was that her father was from the third dimension and her mother from the fourth. And that her evil uncle had driven her mother away, and would someday come for his niece when her mother could no longer protect her. Meleia didn't know why. She didn't understand anything. Her mother had said she would, on her eighteenth birthday. But that was still two years in the future. She needed to know it all now. Now, when her very life was at stake.

I have to find a way out of this room! Meleia wiped her face and lifted her head. She tried to push herself upright but it felt as though the room tilted around her and she sank back to the floor with a groan. Her whole body throbbed, one pounding pulse of pain with each heartbeat. Despair swept through her. Her uncle had really hurt her. How would she ever be able to escape if she couldn't even sit up? Tears welled again but she forced them down. She couldn't afford to be weak, not now.

Think, Meleia. There has to be a way out of this.

She lay on the floor, huddled in the blanket, staring at the space beneath the bed as she thought about the nearly empty room. The bedsheets would do her no good, nor would the blanket. The thick bedposts were as big around as her thigh—unbreakable. She doubted she could pick up the unwieldy mattress, and little bits of straw would be of no help at all. And what good would the table behind the bed be?

Meleia froze. Table behind the bed? There was no table in the room, much less behind the bed. The headboard stood at the edge of the floor, a mere inch from the invisible wall. Was she hallucinating?

She blinked her eyes clear and peered again beneath the bed. There it was, a table, in the space between the headboard and the floor, a slab of thick hand-hewn wood. Part of a table, anyway, sitting close to her side of the bed where the floor and invisible wall met. She couldn't see the side edges of the table, they broke off abruptly into darkness that stretched out to each side. But there was a partial tabletop there, in just that one spot.

"What?" Meleia whispered.

She reached under the bed to touch the table and felt not rough wood but a smooth, cold surface beneath her fingers. Glass? And suddenly her mind deciphered what her

eyes were seeing: a jagged shiny oblong of glass roughly 8"
by 12" leaning up against the invisible wall beneath the
bed's headboard. She traced the outer edge of the glass.
Pain arrowed down her fingers and she gasped, pulled her
hand away. Blood welled on her fingertips. Broken glass,
then, an opaque surface that only faintly reflected her hand,
her arm.

A piece of a mirror? If so, then where was the table?

She twisted, looked behind her. No table. Then she
pushed herself up off the floor and looked around the
room. No table. Just a bed. No walls, no doorway, no table.

Am I crazy? she wondered. Then she looked at the
blood on her fingertips. No, there definitely was something
mirror-like under the bed. But not like any mirror she'd ever
seen. What it reflected didn't seem to be in this room.

She lay down on the floor again and inched partway
under the bed for a closer look at the image in the mirror.
Beyond the table she glimpsed stone walls, the corner of a
rough bench and the hint of a fireplace to the left. No
windows, just part of a crude, iron-bound wooden door. She
couldn't see any ceiling and only a bit of the floor. A young
man stood near the door, half-turned away from her. A
broom made from twigs lay at his feet. He kept glancing
toward her—or perhaps at the table—from the corner of his
eye. He wore a long-sleeve green tunic and dark brown
pants she thought might be made of leather. His brown hair
sparked red in the lamplight. Meleia again reached out and
touched the glass, leaving behind a smear of red. The young
man frowned, then turned and took a few cautious steps
closer to the table. He raised his head and looked directly at
her with eyes the color of old amber. And her heart turned
over.

* * *

Shock shuddered through Emril's body when he saw that the drape, in place since his mother had died, had fallen from the long, oval Oracle-glass hanging on the wall. And there was someone in there. Not a whole image; the shard in the other room wasn't large enough to show much more than an arm and a head.

He dropped his broom and stared. A girl. Lying on the floor, crying, wrapped in a tattered blanket. He shook his head and backed away. Denial filled his chest with each intake of breath. This wasn't right. He shouldn't be seeing her, shouldn't be seeing anyone in this glass. It was his mother's; no one else should be using it, should be able to use it.

He winced as his mother's long-ago words echoed in his head: Those who see more than themselves in the Oracle-glass must help those who appear to them. It is their destiny. Again, he shook his head. No. Not him. He'd seen his mother all those years ago, and he hadn't been able to help her. There was no way he was going to help someone else. It wasn't fair. His mother was dead because of him, and for all he cared, everyone else could die, too. It wasn't his responsibility anymore, no matter what he saw in the glass.

He clenched his jaw and tried to turn away. But he couldn't, not fully. He peered at the girl in the mirror from the corner of his eye as he remembered the night the guards had come to drag his mother to the Regent. Emril, seven years old then, had been the man of the house. It was his responsibility to protect his mother. He'd gone after the guards when they'd come for her, his only weapon the heavy iron skillet he'd snatched from the cook stove. And though he could barely lift it, he'd managed to wound one of the vile men. Not by hitting him with the pan, but by scalding him with the hot oil that had filled the skillet. Then another of the guards had backhanded him across the room. The last thing he'd heard before he'd lost consciousness was his mother's scream.

She'd never come home. The Regent had locked her in his personal prison, the aerie dungeon. Emril's only contact with her was through the glass, six years of silent communing as his mother's captor tried to break her down. Then one day the Regent, visiting Arlenda, had somehow seen Emril in what should have been, to him, a plain mirror. The monster had known it for what it was. He'd smashed the Oracle-glass in the dungeon room, snapping the mother-son link and thereby destroying Arlenda's strong spirit. Not long after that Emril had glimpsed her still, lifeless form in the one shard that remained undiscovered. From that moment on he'd covered the huge oval glass and kept a profile lower than the slugs that crawled in the garden outside. It was never safe to come to the Regent's notice, not for any reason.

He sidled over to the glass, intrigued despite himself. The girl lay on the floor paying him no attention, her face awash with tears, a red welt raised on one cheek. Blood from a swollen lip stained her pale skin and slim fingers. Long black hair tangled around her head and shoulders. She looked to be about his age. Who was she? What had she done to merit the aerie?

She swiped at her wet face with a shaking hand and Emril shook his head. Yes, she'd been hurt. The mark on her face and blood on her lip told him that. But she shouldn't be lying there, crying like a baby. His mother had never cried, not once in all the years that she'd been locked in that room, no matter what the Regent had done to her, things far worse than a blow on the cheek and a split lip. His mother had been strong, resilient. She'd never given in. But this girl? She was a weakling, not worth the effort of helping. She probably deserved her imprisonment. Emril felt the tension in his gut begin to relax.

Then the girl's eyes blinked. He watched recognition flood her face and knew she'd seen his room, perhaps even seen him. But how? Not just anyone could recognize the power of the Oracle-glass.

He watched her eyes widen with disbelief. Her mouth dropped open. She reached out, then gasped and pulled her hand back. Blood welled on her fingertips. She twisted to look behind her and a moment later her head and shoulders disappeared as she pushed herself up and turned around. Then she lay down on the floor again and slid closer to her room's shard of Oracle-glass. Hope flared in her eyes, huge deep violet eyes that appeared fathomless and far wiser than her age.

Emril took a step forward, drawn by those intriguing eyes. The girl reached out a tentative hand, touched the shard, left a smear of red behind. Her mouth opened in a gasp. She leaned closer to the glass just as he lifted his head and looked directly at her. Their eyes met and Emril's world fell apart. He could read the words on her lips, just as he'd been able to read his mother's.

Help me.

Emril's heart stuttered. A low keen of anguish erupted from his throat. Shaking, he stooped, picked up the cloth and flung it over the glass on his wall. Not me, he thought. Never. Not me. If he couldn't help his mother, there was no way he'd help anyone else. No matter how appealing her eyes were.

COFFIN OF SILENCE

She lay on her back in the darkened bedroom beside her husband, listening to the silence. Not until Donald's sleep was deep enough would she move. Eyes wide on eight years of memories, she measured his breathing against the thudding of her heart. *If I don't go*, she thought, *if I fall asleep and don't go, what will Curt do? Go away?* Her breath caught in her throat at the hope, though she knew in her heart its futility. Curt would never go away.

The bedsprings creaked. Donald turned onto his side, facing her. She closed her eyes and tried to regulate her ragged breathing. It cut into the silence, broke it into tiny useless fragments, and that scared her. She needed silence. It was her only ally, the one thing that kept her safe. Her eyes began to burn, and she opened them again.

Turning her head on the too-warm pillow she studied the bedside clock. Black hands stood stark against the sickly green glow of the dial, reminding her of the iron nails she'd found once, in a field where an old barn had stood. Handmade nails; square heads, angular sides, rough-hewn points still sharp after years in the ground. Pointed, like the hands of the clock slicing through her safety net of time. It was time to go.

She looked at Donald once more, then carefully folded back the covers and slid from the bed. Moonlight barred through half-open blinds; the closet door creaked when she eased it open. She froze, heart thudding. Moonlight zebra-striped her body with silver light. Donald slept on like a child, trusting the night and the silence to bring him once again into a new day. She wasn't sure which one of them was the fool.

She reached into the closet and eased clothing from two hangers. The metal frames clanged together, shattering the stillness like breaking glass. She clamped a trembling hand on them and held her breath. Her pounding heart added to the metallic echo. Surely Donald would hear and wake. But he merely turned onto his other side, facing away from her. She crossed to her dresser, eased a drawer ajar, and slipped delicate underthings from within.

She went into the adjoining bath where, with only the dim glow of a nightlight for company, she pushed the negligee straps off her wide shoulders. The gown puddled around her feet, silken folds glistening in the faint light. She pulled on panties first, delicate fabric that slid up with a whisper and settled snug around her hips. High-cut legs and lots of lace; very feminine. She let her graceful hands, long nails lacquered a burnished copper, rove over the smooth expanse of her abdomen and down across her pubic mound, reveling in the flatness. She sighed, wishing this weren't happening, and turned again to her clothes.

Should she wear a bra? She glanced at the lace and elastic concoction draped on the edge of the tub, then looked at her reflection in the mirror over the sink. No. She wanted him to see what she had done, what it meant. He had to realize that this was not a game, not for her. It was her life.

She drew cool linen slacks of burnt orange up her legs. As usual, the clasp at the waist gave her trouble. There were some things she would never get used to. *Moving away wasn't enough. I should have changed my name, too*, she thought, slipping a pale apricot silk shell over her head. Its creamy caress rippled through her, making her shiver.

Dark brown sandals next, sloping wedged soles adding another two inches to her five-foot-seven-inch stature. *Tall for a woman, which is good,* she thought, sidling through the door into the bedroom, *but short for a man, which isn't. How strange that right and wrong can be determined by something as simple as gender.*

She looked at the bed. Donald slept deeply, unaware that she was no longer beside him, oblivious to the danger that threatened them. If he found out, he would leave her. And if she lost him, she would die. Her existence would have no meaning without Donald. Straight-laced, morally rigid Donald.

"I love you," she whispered, and left the bedroom.

The night was cool and clear. A soft breeze kissed the ground; twinkling stars studded black velvet above. A half-moon shed pale silvery light across the landscape. She steered Donald's Porsche out of the city. A gym bag nestled on the bucket seat beside her, a brown vinyl envelope purse atop it. Disposable, all of it, purchased expressly for this night. She had planned carefully, knew what she had to do. There was no room for surprise. She couldn't afford any, not now. Not when life was finally worth living.

Far from civilization, the car bounced down an overgrown dirt track. She parked deep in the shadow of an ancient oak and studied the long-abandoned farm buildings. Stars glimmered through gaps in siding and roofs. Ghosts flitting in the dark shadows were the only moving things in sight. A rusty old station wagon stood a dozen feet away. *So he's here*, she thought. *Let's get this over with.* She checked her purse and got out of the car. She scanned the darkness around her, then slung the chain strap onto her shoulder and walked toward the chicken run crumbling between house and barn.

He was there, cigarette end glowing red in the darkness like a manic evil eye. Twenty feet separated them when she stopped, her mouth suddenly dry. They stared at each other in silence. Finally, without taking his eyes off hers, he dropped the cigarette, ground it beneath a booted toe and stepped closer.

"Well, well, well," he sneered. "Just look at you. Robin Sidowski." His gaze dropped down her lean, wiry body, then returned to the hands that held the purse clutched to her stomach. "Oh. Excuse me. I should have said Robin *Berlys*, shouldn't I? Mrs. Donald Berlys. God, what a crock."

The contempt in his tone stabbed into her. He was spoiling for a fight. This wasn't going to be easy. She'd forgotten how intimidating his solid six feet could be. But she didn't rise to his bait. She merely glanced down at the wedding ring sparkling in soft moonglow and returned her gaze to his.

"Did you bring it?" he asked.

"Did you?"

"It's here," he replied, pulling a large Manila envelope from beneath his windbreaker. "Not that it matters, most of this is public record. Anyone has access to it."

"But only you would know to look," she said, unable to keep the bitterness from her tone.

He cocked an eyebrow. She stepped forward, lips parted, right hand stretching for the envelope. He lifted it above his head, just out of her reach.

"Uh-uh. The money first."

"And when you get it, you'll go away and never come back again, right?"

His sharp gaze raked her body once again, catching on her breasts, on silk-covered nipples peaked from the chill air.

"Maybe." His voice was so low she could barely hear it. "I think I'm changing my mind."

"What the hell does that mean?"

"It means I'd start saving my money, if I were you."

His thin lips stretched in a ghoulish smile. Moonlight painted his pale hair silver, turned the down on her arms, never very dark and lighter now, to glistening white. Robin turned her head and bit her lip. She had never hated him more than she did right now.

"If you get greedy, Curt, I'll kill you."

"You?" He snorted. "You wouldn't have the guts. You run from your problems. Well, the running's over now. You owe me, Robin, and you'll pay. Once a year."

"No." She tried to say it forcefully, but her voice broke. It came out quaking with fear.

"Oh, yes, once a year. Shit, it won't cause you any real hardship. Your precious Donald makes a mint and you're practicing again. You can afford it. How does twenty-five grand a year sound? Pretty damn cheap for silence, don't you agree, *Mrs.* Berlys?"

She looked at him, took a step closer on trembling legs, and shook her head. "Why are you doing this to me?"

"Because you betrayed me! You betrayed us and what we were." His left hand fisted, ready to strike. His anger left her breathless. "I loved you. God, Robbie, you *knew* how much I loved you! We belonged together. Everything was perfect. Then you did... this!"

"It wasn't easy for me, Curt. I lost everything, too."

"Not for long!" He grabbed her arm and pulled her close, his fingers cruelly tight. Robin gasped and cowered away from the snarling face that loomed over her. "Did you even *think* of me, of what this would do to me? Did you even *care* how I'd feel? You made a mockery of me, turned our love into something sick, putrid. And look at what you've become." He let her go with a little shove; she stumbled back a step. "My God, you're disgusting. Obscene. It makes me sick to think that I touched you, that I made love to you. How can you stand living with yourself every day?"

"I-I'm sorry, Curt." Despite her resolve to stay strong, Robin felt shaken by the depth of his pain. "I didn't mean to hurt you, I really didn't. I tried to make you understand, you know that. Pretending wasn't enough. It was tearing me apart. I had to do it. I was so unhappy. I had needs—"

"Well, so do I! I need money and you're going to give it to me. As much as I want, whenever I want it. Or your precious Donald will learn a few fascinating facts about his sweet, lovely little wife."

He tucked the Manila envelope beneath his left arm and glared at her, his right hand extended palm up. Robin stared back a moment then nodded, zipped open her purse, and fumbled inside with her right hand. The corner of a thick white envelope appeared; she grasped it with her left hand and laid it on Curt's palm. Her right hand stayed in her purse.

"Is it all here?"

Robin shrugged. "Count it if you don't trust me."

Curt bent his head and opened the envelope. Robin took a step closer to him.

"Good-bye, Curt," she whispered.

He looked up, frowned. She fired the revolver at point-blank range; two shots through the vinyl of the purse and the nylon of his windbreaker, the cotton of his shirt, through skin and muscle, into his heart. Curt's mouth dropped open. Shock widened his eyes. He staggered back two paces, three. The envelopes fell to the dusty ground. He tried to speak, to call her name; no sound emerged. He shook his head, his last conscious movement. Then his knees buckled, and he dropped to the ground. His breath sighed out in rattling protest, and he lay still.

Robin picked up the two envelopes and carried them to the Porsche. Removing faded jeans and an old sweatshirt from the gym bag, she changed quickly. She doubted that anyone had heard the shots; there was no one within half a mile of the old farm, and the purse had muffled the noise. Slinging the gym bag onto her shoulder, she dragged Curt's body back to the old well behind the barn. Luckily, her strength had not diminished much; within three minutes she shifted the heavy wooden well cover and tipped the bloodstained body into the silent black depths. Wiping sweat from her brow, she opened the gym bag once again.

The nails were cold in her mouth; their metallic taste triggered her saliva. The moon had sunk lower in the sky. It elongated her shadow across the well cover, a mute, ebony companion. One by one she rammed the nails home, sealing the well shut, forming it into a secret, dark, silent coffin. As the nails pierced her shadow's outline, she thought of Peter Pan sewing his shadow in place. When she left, would hers be left behind, held fast by the same nails that secured the silence of her life?

She pounded the last nail deep into the wood and sat back on her heels, listening to the stillness of the land around her, the bitter taste of the nails lingering on her tongue. She saw Curt's face on the flat wooden cover, washed gray by the sickly light. She hadn't realized how ugly death was, how cold and final. When she rose and returned to her car, she did not look back to see if her shadow followed.

The house was dark and silent. She listened at the bottom of the stairs for a moment, heard nothing, then went into the study. She lit a small fire and, kneeling before the hearth; she opened the manila envelope and spilled its contents onto the bricks. One by one she fed the papers into the blaze, her hand moving back and forth, each crackling flame another nail in her coffin of silence. Newspaper clippings; she had no need to read them; they were seared into her brain. 'Transvestite Attorney "De-Frocked"; Assistant D.A. Sidowski Dismissed.' One by one they curled into ash; papers, letters, photographs. And at the very bottom, a copy of her birth certificate.

Dark smoke wafted up the chimney. Stray sparks leapt up to join it. An odd smell emanated from the flames; cold, damp and rot, the odor of the well, the aroma of silence. At last she rose, took the poker and probed the ashes, making sure no trace of the past remained. Her secret was safe again, the silence inviolate. *Until the next time*, Curt's voice whispered as she slowly climbed the stairs. *It's all public record, even your birth certificate.*

Robin Lesley Sidowski. Born at 9:33 pm on April 15, 1974, to Robert and Mary Sidowski. Seven pounds six ounces, 20 inches long. Sex: *male*.

Until the operation. Eight long years ago.

By the soft glow of the bathroom nightlight, she slid the long satin negligee over her head. It settled around her with a shimmer, and she thought of the silent starlit water that had closed over the weighted gym bag. She felt hollow and empty. Panic lay somewhere deep inside, screaming for release it could never have. Trembling, she stepped into the bedroom.

Everything was as she had left it, dim and quiet. Donald slept on, flat and dead-looking in the pallid light, though she could hear him breathe. Dead; Robin's breath caught in her throat. She crossed the room quickly to slide in beside him, clinging desperately to a protective silence pierced now by echoes of her heartbeat, Curt's soft whisper, the metallic ring of the hammer. The laddering moonlight had shifted.

Blood-dark shadows now slashed across the bed where they lay alone, side by side, phantom nails impaling her breast, her belly, pinning her life to the mattress. She couldn't move. Eyes burning, she lay staring at the dark ceiling, drowning in silence, waiting for daylight to free her. She could still taste cold iron on her tongue.

AB INITIO

The milk is all gone. I cannot feed the baby. It will die without food, and I am the source. There must be other options, but from my place, chained deep in the dark cave, I cannot see any but the one indisputable, immutable fact. The milk is gone.

I hold the frail infant close to my sweating body, fever bright within the deep, moist depths of my being, and I pray to squeeze out one last drop of sustenance for the child. Perhaps osmosis will pass my life into it, though I have only an intuitive grasp of what that is. But there is so little life left in me, I have none to spare. Only thoughts remain, an over-abundance of words and images crowding my brain: Years of growth, of learning; first teeth, first steps, first laugh; first words of love murmured into a girlfriend's ear. Firsts that now will never be.

I know that it is not fair that this child, this piece of my heart, my soul, my flesh, should die simply because I cannot fight the sickness, have not the strength in me to hold on until it no longer has need of me. But nothing in life is fair, however much I rail at fate. And what will be happens as it will, without my input or agreement.

I wanted so much for you, I tell the baby, stroking its silky head with fingers shaking from weakness. *I wanted life, love, happiness, freedom; all the things I have never had.* It will be a bond that always ties us, I know, a connection forged from want and privation instead of joy and fulfillment. And although this bond is not fair, it has to be enough for me. It is all I will ever have.

I lay my head back on the dank, cold stone as my eyesight dims. And He approaches, dragging with him another captive woman, a woman with terrified eyes, whose torn blouse reveals weeping breasts. My chest contracts, my desiccated flesh dry-heaving in empathy. My arms tighten on the child, and He pulls hard enough to rouse his son to wails. He thrusts the infant at the new woman, shoves the child's face into her body, her breast, and with an anguished cry she clasps it to her nipple and lets her sorrow flood his belly.

He thrusts his son's new milk source to the ground and wraps a chain around her ankle. I wonder if she will be kind to my child, if her milk is sweet, and if, unlike me, she will live long enough to nourish the child into full life.

The man bends and caresses the boy's head. The baby blinks, lets go of the nipple, looks up at his father. And in my child's face I see the future; another such as this man, his mirror image. As my life force drains away, I pray the new milk will sour.

FAIR GAME

I had never seen my dad cry before. I didn't even know he was capable of tears. Mom, yes, she cried all the time, especially when Dad hit her. Or me. But not Dad. He never cried.

But there he stood, spotlit by the lights from the police car, his wet face glistening in the brightness as a river poured out of each eye. You'd think the world had just come to an end, though maybe for him it had. Me? I'd never understand why anyone would care so much. Or want to care.

I mean, it was just a car, for heaven's sake. It had four tires, two doors, what Dad called a rag top and one steering wheel. Just like all the other cars on the road. So what if it was worth a fortune, as he told the lead detective? So what if it was one of a kind? He had insurance, didn't he?

He hadn't cried when my brother took the easy way out of the family. They found Josh at the quarry two years ago, though he hadn't drowned. He'd taken something, I don't know what, and just lay on the cold sand until he turned cold. Every time I entered a room for months afterward, all conversation would stop. Maybe they thought if I knew how to get out, I'd do it, too. Stupid people.

I'm smarter than that. I waded through Mom's tears, her self-recriminations, her selfish concentration on what she had lost. She never once thought about me, what I had lost: my only brother, my best friend, the buffer between Dad and me. With Josh gone, I was fair game. Dad told me so, with every slap, every punch, every beating. I could have left, just run away, but if I was fair game, I was willing to stick around and find the fairness. It was only right.

Took two years, until the local hoodlums smashed into Dad's antique BMW convertible. And I found out what could hurt him. I had to turn away, pretend to be upset also, in order to hide my smile. Because I knew my Dad. I knew what was precious to him. Not what should be; his family, his wife and daughter. No, what mattered were his things.

I know lots of people at school who would do anything for a few bucks. The plan burst into my head fully clothed, with only a slight adjustment needed here and there. So, when the detective came up to me and asked me if I'd seen anything, I just shook my head.

"I was in my room," I said. True, though I didn't tell him Dad had locked me in the closet. I'd been in there for about seven hours until he let me out, afraid of what might happen if the cops looked around inside and discovered me. "Sorry."

Except I wasn't. I stood watching the worst thing Dad had ever gone through and made my mental list. This was only the beginning. A surprise beginning, a serendipitous beginning, to be sure, but a beginning nonetheless. I was about to become Dad's worst, but invisible, nightmare.

I think I'll start with his antique grandfather clock.

EDUCATION

"**Did** you look at her fingers?" Billy asked me.

"Huh?"

I stared at him, drink in hand. I was half blitzed already, and we'd only been at the party about an hour. Everything had a nice wavering aura around it, and sound echoed as from the bottom of a deep well. All around me nubile flesh clad in very little pranced and danced, one of the major perks to college life. The last thing I wanted to do, or even thought of doing, was look at someone's fingers.

"Her hands, man." Billy shook his head. "Never seen nothing like that."

I was almost drunk enough to correct his grammar— what other point was there to being a nerdy English major—but someone in the back of the room let out a shriek. It startled me, and I spilled my beer. I sat contemplating the puddle that once was my lap while Billy yammered on.

"It was like a freaking freak show, man. Most amazing thing I ever seen." He took a gulp of his beer, belched loud enough to be heard in Hoboken, and shook his head. "Fingers like freak shows, I kid you not. Freaking freak shows."

He wound down, and we sat in a rare moment of silence. Not rare for me, I've never been more than a two-word Charlie. And not all that rare for Billy, though he often trips over the words that do spill out of his lips. But rare for a room full of liquored-up frat guys surrounded by women in pretty much every stage of undress except complete.

Total silence. For one heartbeat, two beats, three. Then all hell broke loose.

Screams, shouts, shoves, feet climbing the furniture, dishes and glasses shattering on the floor, girls crying and moaning... No, that was Walter-the-jock moaning, Walter on the floor, rolling around like a fish out of water, clutching his red shirt in even redder hands... wait, that shirt was yellow when he arrived, wasn't it?

I sat there and stared as Billy abandoned me and thrust himself through the crowd toward the front door. I heard the front windows break and faster than I could recite the first verse of the Star-Spangled Banner, the frat house was pretty much empty. Except for Walter, still rolling and moaning, though a lot slower now, and a couple of freshman girls who had passed out before I got there.

And there she was, coming toward me from across the room, half-nightmare, half wet-dream. A smile played at the corners of her lips, ruby red luscious lips, lips I wanted to clamp my mouth on and lick. She tilted her head as she got closer, then stopped and looked at the beer-n-shot still in my hand.

"You going to drink that?" she asked.

Her velvet voice slithered down my spine and I shuddered even as I nodded and drank. Then she stepped closer and reached for me, reached with her finger-claws, talons as red as Walter's shirt, as the puddle spreading beneath him.

"I like you," she whispered and let me lick those lips of hers.

The room erupted into rainbows. It crawled around the perimeter of the walls and rocked like a boat on the high seas. She ran a sharp nail down my cheek, then hooked my shirt and pulled me close. Hooked me with those fingers of hers, and I knew I was a goner.

"I think I'll try and keep you," she said as she towed me off the stool and across the room to the staircase.

We began to climb as I contemplated correcting her grammar. Then I realized my days of being an English nerd were over. The hell with grammar; I had taloned fingers to keep me hooked and luscious red lips to lick. Isn't college great?

AS THE TIDE CAME IN

"Ma'am? Is something wrong?"

Carly looked up at the man, a twenty-something, bearded beachcomber in ratty t-shirt, hiking shorts, and boots. And eyes dark with concern, as though he'd watched her pace for a while.

"My son," she said, her breath hitching in her throat. "He went in the cave and hasn't come out. And now the tide is coming in..."

She looked at the dark slit in the cliff face, the seawater washing into the entrance. She'd never thought of the danger. Dozens of kids, beachcombers, even camera buffs explored the cavern daily. They'd posted no barriers, no warnings. Ben had gone in an hour ago. She'd twisted her ankle and cut her feet on the sharp rocks when she'd tried to go after him. Now she was drowning in fear and guilt. What kind of mother couldn't overcome a little pain to save her child? What was wrong with her?

"Do you want me to go in and look for him?" the young man asked.

"You wouldn't mind? Oh, thank you. His name is Ben."

"Don't worry." He laid a warm hand on her shoulder. "We'll be back before you know it."

She watched the young man wade through ankle-deep water and vanish into the cavern, hearing again her son's reluctance when she'd asked him to go geode hunting for her. Ben, at eleven, was small for his age, timid and fearful of other boys' roughhousing. She needed to push him gently, instill confidence, especially since Al had died. It was up to her to raise him into a strong, competent man.

"I don't want to." Ben scowled.

"Please, Ben?" Carly's ankles and feet throbbed from picking her way over the shifting stones and coarse grit that comprised the beach. "You know how I love geodes, and the best ones are in the cave."

"Come with me, Mom."

"I can't, baby. Wrong shoes." She shrugged. "Please, do it for Mommy?"

Ben hunched his shoulders and shook his head.

"Oh, come on, kiddo." She gave him a tiny shove toward the cavern. "You can do it. Go get me a nice big one."

He'd looked at her, sighed, then trudged toward the entrance slit. He turned and waved just before the darkness swallowed him. Carly had smiled. She was glad now she had forgotten her boots. She knew Ben didn't like dark places, but he'd obeyed her anyway. Her little man had overcome yet another hurdle. How many more would there be before he was fully grown?

But the beachcomber couldn't find Ben. Carly stood outside the cave, unable to think, barely able to breathe, feet bloody and heart numb as she watched the young man join the volunteers who flowed in and out of the darkness as day morphed into night into day until Ben's body was found. He'd crawled through a small hole deep in the cavern, gotten stuck and drowned in the onrushing tide. Carly watched it all until they brought her son out. Until they posted warning signs and cordoned off the dangerous parts of the cave. Then she stopped noticing anything.

Ben came to her six months later, in the deep darkness of her despair. Limned in soft light, his face glowed with joy and peace. She cried out and opened her arms, but he just hovered there, a few inches off the floor.

"I'm so sorry, baby," she said, her voice choked, her words barely discernible. "Please, don't hate me."

Ben smiled. *It's okay, Mom. You did right in pushing me. You couldn't know what would happen. I forgive you.*

Tears fell, releasing her back to the world, but her shredded heart remained numb. And she lived on, alone.

Now she'd returned to the cave for the first time since it happened. She stood before the opening and felt again the horror of Ben's death. *Twenty years. How have I survived this long?* she wondered. *Why have I wanted to?* She thought of Ben's gentle smile, heard again his soft comforting voice from so long ago: *I forgive you.*

She lifted the bottle, shook a few pills into her mouth, drank them down. And repeated it until the bottle was empty. Then she sat on the cold, damp stones and watched the tide surge in. She let her tears flow, let the end come. Ben's forgiveness was not enough, because she was at fault. And there was no pardon for that.

ELLIE

Nothing ever worked out the way I hoped it would when I was a kid. Though I suppose you might consider me a kid still, 'cause I just turned 18. Yesterday. Not that anyone remembered. Finally legal, they could prosecute me as an adult now. If those ass wipes could ever find me, that is.

Yeah, yeah, I know. Rude, crude, and a bad attitude. So what? I have issues. With authority, as if you couldn't figure that out yourself. No, don't ask. I don't like to talk about it.

Like I said, nothing ever worked out the way I hoped it would. I wanted to be an only child, but I've got four siblings, alien beings transported to earth just to fuck with my life. I've done more babysitting than a professional nanny—without pay, I might add. Mom seems to think that the slop she calls food is payment enough. As if.

Then I wanted to be tall and willowy, with doe eyes and huge cheekbones and a little bow of a mouth, I could paint red. What did I get? Barely an inch over 5 feet—if I stand on tiptoes—with a round baby face, no cheekbones, a straight slash of an almost lipless mouth, and ears that stick out into the other room. I have to keep getting perms, so I have enough curls to hide them. And God forbid I ever pull my hair back into a pony tail. The kids at school call me Ellie... not a bad nickname until you realize it's short for elephant.

I always wanted my own room, with walls painted a deep lavender—my favorite color—and stuffed animals all over the place, and a desk for my computer setup, and a huge window with a big tree right outside, so I could climb out and meet my boyfriend whenever I wanted. But Jessy and Carla got that room, because it was the biggest, and they had to share so they needed the space. Kurt and Andy share the other bedroom on the second floor—Mom and Dad have a suite on the first floor—so I got stuck with the room up in the attic. Wood walls. No ceiling, just open beams. A tiny window that doesn't open, way above the top of any tree, not that there's any trees close to that side of the house. So I bake in the summer and freeze in the winter and have to climb down a fucking ladder just to use the bathroom. Let me tell you, my life sucks.

But at least Dad doesn't visit me anymore after everyone else is asleep. His knees don't like ladders. I often wonder who he visits now, since Jessy and Carly room together. Maybe if I'd had a roomie, Dad wouldn't have wandered in so much until I moved up here.

I don't have any friends at school, except for Barbara. She's an outcast, too. The boys run after her, grunting like a pig, because she's overweight. I found her behind the hydrangea bushes one day in sixth grade, bawling her eyes out. Don't know why it got to me, maybe it was the look on her face—like she wanted to be anywhere but where she was. I feel like that all the time. So we got to be what I call "situational friends." Situation any different, and we'd never even speak to each other.

I think God hates me. Or the universe does, I'm not sure which. I'm not even sure God really exists. If he does, he's gotta be the stupidest being in all of creation. I mean, why would he create people the way they are? We do nasty things, and stink and fart and throw up and say awful things and no one in his or her right mind would ever make people like that. Or love them. Or maybe I'm just what everyone says I am, a little Ellie who should go live in the zoo and amuse those who have good brains.

I think tomorrow I'll load up that virus I designed and destroy all the US banking records. Then we'll see who's smart, huh?

TOUGH BLOOD
Skylark Novel #1 in Progress.

Chapter I

Wake *me when it's over.*
Problem is, it's never over.

I don't particularly like insurance fraud cases, but with my bottom line I wasn't in a position to turn down fairly easy, lucrative work just because it didn't suit my sensibilities. And this guy, Mitchell Argus, was a real slime ball; one of those no-witness, slip-and-fall injuries that didn't result in any pictorial evidence—i.e., x-ray proof— that drained insurance company coffers and raised rates for everyone. I'd almost caught him on film yesterday, but a van drove between us before I could snap his non-crutch-assisted steps, which was why I was on Argus again today, sitting outside Trader Joe's with camera in hand, waiting for him to exit the store. Maybe, since he'd have to juggle grocery bags as well as crutches, fate would smile on me, and I could digitally immortalize his fakery then find that bathroom that had been calling me for the last fifteen minutes.

And fate, that lovely lady, did smile. TJ's door swung open and out strode Argus, three heavy bags in his hands and one set of crutches balanced across his shoulder. I grinned and raised the camera, tweaked the focus, and moved my finger toward the button.

Then fate quit smiling.

My Jeep door was flung open and a pair of meaty hands grabbed me and yanked me out of the car. The camera tumbled onto the ground.

"Got you, sweetheart." The deep growl gouged into me. A huge ape towered over my five-feet-eleven-and-a-half inches and outweighed me by about seventy pounds. "You're under arrest. And you ain't getting out, not ever."

He spun me around. Cold metal clamped tight around my wrists.

"Hey!" I yelped. "What the hell? That hurts!"

"So what? Getting a little of your own back is a good thing, I'd say."

"Who the hell are you? Why are you doing this?" I twisted and bucked in his hard grasp. "Let me go, you cretin!"

"Shut the fuck up," the suit snarled, and shook me like I was a wet dishrag. We stood surrounded by his goon squad, all with guns pointed at little old, trussed-up me like I was still some kind of threat. "I don't wanna hear one more squawk outta you. I'll duck tape your mouth if you say another word. You got that?"

He wrestled me over to the huddle of squad cars blocking traffic in the parking lot. I bit back a cry of pain, hoping my shoulder didn't dislocate—again. Then he pulled open the back door of a county-supplied plain-clothes vehicle that fooled nobody and shoved me in, accidentally-on-purpose forgetting to push my head down. I spent most of the ride to the cop shop with blood trickling down my face and my brain on fire, trying to blink stars out of my vision and praying I'd throw up on his fake leather seat.

I decided compliance was the better part of valor at this point—at least until I unleashed my lawyer on him—and kept my mouth shut as ordered.

He brought me all the way back to the Sheriff's substation in Los Osos from where he'd snatched me in San Luis Obispo; just my luck he was county affiliated and not part of SLO's local police force. That made for a torturous twenty-minute drive east instead of the four or five minute in-town journey it might have been.

I couldn't stifle a few grunts of pain as he hauled me out of the back seat once we arrived, though I managed—barely—not to call his ancestry or intelligence into question. Not out loud, anyway. Then he muscled me through the front door and into the bowels of the station, his hands not any gentler than they'd been thus far. He shoved me into the interrogation room, secured the cuffs to a chair bolted to the floor, and walked out, slamming the door behind him.

All without saying one word to me. No enlightenment as to why I'd been invited to this little shindig. No explanation about the cuffs. Or the mauling. Or the "under arrest" crap. Just abuse and silence as an intimidation tactic.

As if. Takes more than a battering from a Neanderthal ape to intimidate me. I rolled my aching shoulders to try to ease the stress—not that it helped much—and pretended I was anywhere but in that room.

The handcuffs had been cinched tight enough to cut through skin and scrape against bone as I'd been hauled into and out of the squad car. I was pretty sure the moisture I felt on my fingers wasn't sweat. My shoulders burned from the way my arms were pulled behind my back. I waited for Ape-man-the-cop to come back in so I could demand answers. And unleash the "L" word. Not that lawyers are any better than cops, but through experience I've discovered that mentioning my particular "L" word makes law enforcement types shudder in their boots.

I sat there alone as the afternoon ticked away, eyes closed, practicing visualization and doing deep breathing exercises for what I estimated was at least two hours, pretty sure Ape-man and his cronies stood watching behind the one-way glass, hoping for a meltdown. What they would get was a lawsuit once I got Maureen into the mix. I knew I hadn't done anything—not for a while, anyway—so I was more pissed than scared. I just wanted to get this mistaken identity thing over with, so I could go home to where that bottle of Glenlivet was waiting for me. And where I could get out of my stupid bra. I spent part of the time composing a report in my head that explained why I hadn't finished the surveillance on Argus, though I had to get a bit creative since I hadn't any idea what had caused this particular delay. And I spent the other part of it wishing I didn't have to pee so badly. I doubted Ape-man would uncuff me for a restroom visit no matter how politely I asked. I could just hear his response...

As *soon as you confess, sweetheart, I'll have you taken to the bathroom.*

Said, I was sure, with those beady eyes shining, a sadistic grin on those thick lips, and pure malice in his tone.

Rats. Another deep breath and more visualization exercises, ones that didn't include water of any kind.

The pain in my head, shoulders and wrists was starting to impinge on my Zen state when the door finally swung open. In walked Ape-man, accompanied by a shorter, slimmer, younger, black-haired detective of obvious Hispanic heritage. He moved with catlike grace, reminding me of a leopard. Ape-man sat opposite me and slapped a folder on the stained Formica tabletop. Leopard situated himself against the wall, arms crossed, eyes lapping up every nuance of my body language. Ape-man opened the folder.

Let the games begin, I thought.

"Skylark," he said in his deep grating rasp. "Skylark. Huh. What kind of weirdo name is that?"

The one Social Services saddled me with, I thought as I stared into his narrowed, calculating eyes. Since he'd so politely requested I remain mute, I didn't grace him with an audible reply.

"And no last name either, just plain old Skylark. Guess you think that makes you special. Better than the rest of us. I know," he snapped his fingers then pointed a thick index finger at me, "maybe you're like another Cher, or Madonna. A real 'freaky' one." He air quoted freaky. "Hey, we got us a celebrity here, José."

He grinned his sarcasm at Leopard—who grinned his own back—looked at the paper again, then up at me, face now flooded with scorn.

"Haven't had no last name, not since, let's see," again he looked down and appeared to read for a few moments, not that I for a second believed he needed to, "you turned eighteen and went and had it erased. Before that it was... let's see... *Friday*. Skylark *Friday*. You believe that one, José?" He turned eyes filled with incredulity on his partner, who shook his head.

"Not in this lifetime," Leopard purred.

Ape-man turned back to me.

"Skylark *Friday*," he repeated, again emphasizing my last name. "Sounds made up, you ask me."

I didn't ask, I thought, but again forbore to respond aloud to his ridicule. Since he'd somehow gotten hold of sealed records, he already knew I'd been named by the state of California which, in its infinite non-wisdom, took my last name from the day I'd been discovered on the steps of the Los Angeles Social Services building. Without once considering what it would do to me, coupled as it was with my odd first name. I was closing in on thirty and still not over the teasing I'd endured all through school.

"Sky-lark Fri-day, Sky-lark Fri-day." Ape-man crooned the syllables like they were the latest romance ballad. "Skylark Friday... Oooh, that would make you a *girl Friday*, wouldn't it? You work alone, or are you some guy's *girl Friday*, huh? Do whatever he wants, like a good little *girl Friday*? Do all the dirty work for him? Or are you just dirty all on your own?"

I kept my head bowed, my stare on the scarred table top. My jaw ached from grinding my teeth. Ape-man was damned lucky my arms were still fastened behind my back, or he'd not have a face left. How the hell had he opened sealed records? What was going on here? Just what the hell had I been arrested for? I almost asked, almost opened my mouth, but when I lifted my head and saw the look of cunning on Leopard's face I decided not to give either one of them any satisfaction.

Ape-man turned a page and again pretended to read. I squirmed in pain and seized the moment.

"You gonna take these cuffs off any time soon?"

"Depends." He looked up at me and grinned. "You gonna sit there nice and quiet like a good little girl?"

That did it. It was past time to show this Neanderthal ape just who he was dealing with.

"No." I stared unblinking into his eyes, ignored the way my hands itched to teach him a lesson in civility, and let my snark ooze out in a quiet, measured tone. "I'm going to sit here quietly like the adult woman I am and watch you preen, and pose, and act like the adolescent asshole you are." Leopard snorted a laugh and Ape-man's face reddened. Steam shot from his ears. "*And* wait for my lawyer to show up," I added just as he started to speak.

The magic "L" word seemed to stop him cold. He stared at me a moment, blinked his beady eyes then, to my surprise, burst into derisive laughter.

"Ohhh, I'm so scared. José, she said the "L" word!"

"I want my phone call," I said.

I'd intended it put all the scorn and anger I felt behind the words, but the pain bouncing around in my body weakened my voice, and it came out sounding a bit shaky. With an underlying pleading whine, I could have done without.

Ape-man turned another page, then slapped a huge palm on the paper.

"Tell you what, you tell me why you killed this guy, and I'll let you use the phone."

This is about a murder? I shook my head.

"What are you talking about? What guy? What murder? I haven't killed anyone."

I knew it was a mistake when I saw the way his eyes lit up. I should have stuck with the "L" word and not engaged him at all, but somehow my mouth got ahead of my mind. Pain does that to me, sometimes.

Ape-man's eyes grew big. His brows rose. His mouth opened into a disbelieving "O"—a fairly well-feigned proximation of incredulity given his bull-in-a-china-shop personality. Behind him, Leopard sucked in his cheeks to hold back a grin.

"Haven't killed *anyone*? Not *ever*? What about that Kaiser fella, what was his name?" Ape-man glanced at, then tapped, the file. "Pietr. That's it. Man, you carved him up good, sweetheart. Not much left of him once you was done, was there?"

"That was self-defense," I said, my teeth clenched with rage. "He attacked me first, and I have the scars to prove it."

"Ohhh, I'd *love* to see *those*."

His beady eyes inspected my body like his mind was busy undressing me. I turned my head away and closed my eyes. After a moment of trying to unnerve me—it didn't work, he wasn't that good at lascivious leering—he went on, naming a few more turds I'd had run-ins with over the last seven years. I hate the more violent aspects of being a P.I., which is why, now that I was finally on my own, I specialized mostly in corporate cases with their nice, clean, non-violent computer searches. Not that it stopped the area's underbelly from stepping on me every once in a while; being a woman in what is traditionally a man's occupation just brings out the best in some people. So there'd been times I'd been forced to use my fists. Or my Glock. Each encounter left me riddled with either guilt or ghosts.

Then Ape-man went one too far.

"And let's not forget little Billy Cranston."

A wave of heat washed over me. I could feel Vesuvius begin to rumble deep within. I opened my eyes and looked daggers at him.

"I never hurt Billy." I forced the words through stiff, numb lips. "He killed himself."

"Yeah, because you hounded him to death."

"You son of a—"

I snapped my mouth shut and glared at this cretin of a man who sat blank-faced, staring at me with a glint of expectation and triumph in his hazel eyes. The pain of failing Billy roared through me like a tsunami. If the chair hadn't been bolted to the floor, the way my body shuddered from rage would have walked it across the room.

"Oh, my, my. That hit a nerve. Didn't it, *Skylark Friday*?" Ape-man purred. It took all my strength to unlock my jaw enough to force out words.

"Where's. My. Lawyer?"

Ape-man made a big show of looking around the room, then ducking to check under the table. He turned to look at Leopard.

"You know where her lawyer is, José?"

"Nope." Leopard shrugged his own feigned ignorance. "Not a clue."

"You hear her ask *for* her lawyer, José?"

"Nope. Just where hers was."

Ape-man turned back to me and shook his head.

"I'm astounded. *Your* lawyer, not *a* lawyer? You actually got one on call? Just like a real celebrity criminal... Wow. How the hell do you afford your very own shyster mouthpiece? You dealing drugs outta that office of yours?"

I closed my eyes; it took a count of seven before I could open them again and speak without telling Ape-man and Leopard where they could go, and what they could do to themselves once they got there.

"I want my lawyer, now," I said, enunciating each word with clipped precision. "I want to confer with my lawyer, Maureen Overton, before we go any further. I am asking for my lawyer. Call Maureen Overton, now. I will not speak to you until I have conferred with Ms. Overton. Is that *clear enough* for you, *Detective*?"

Ape-man stared at me for a long moment, emotions flitting across his face so fast I couldn't decipher them, ending with disgust that stayed and twisted his thick features. Then he closed the file.

"The Overton is your lawyer?" He pursed his lips and shook his head. "I should have known."

Then he rose, and the two detectives left the room, slamming the door behind them, leaving me alone, in increasing pain, and still tethered to the chair.

<u>SECTION FIVE</u>

C.B. Taylor

Original Artwork by Christine B. Taylor

For as long as I can remember, I have been a storyteller. As a kid with a pencil and a lined notebook, I drew wordless comic book adventures for my brothers. As an adult with a smartphone, I wrote dialogue as fast as my fingers could tap, during live international fiction events on Twitter.

As much as I love art and writing on their own, it's in storytelling that my favorite crafts really come to life. "Storytelling" isn't solitary—it implies an audience, a collaboration; someone else participates in the tale, through their imagination or with words of their own.

I'm thrilled that the next chapter in my career will give me a chance to collaborate with four of the best storytellers I know. Watch for Tales from a Rocky Coast: Volume II—and bring your imagination!

mousewords.com   mousewords.tumblr

AUTHORS' CONTACT INFORMATION AND BOOKS

B. Carter Pittman

Photo by B. Carter Pittman

Finding Carter:

Website:

bcarterpittman.fridaynightwritersgroup.com

Publications:

Memoirs:

Take Flight: Byzantium
Vol. 18, Pages 84 - 91.
Willy and the Cyclone
(Editors' Choice Award)

Anthologies:

Reflections of Light
The National Library of Poetry. Page 452: The
Difference. (1995).

Best Poems of 1996. The National Library of Poetry.
Page 124: Mortal Man. (1996).

Tellus Magazine. The Cuesta College Literary Journal,
10th Edition. Pages 22 - 26. Fudging. (2002)

Tales from The Corner, an Anthology. Central Coast
Press. Pages 21 - 28. Circles. (2005)

Tales from The Corner, an Anthology. Central Coast
Press. Page 80. Ad Infinitum. (2005)

Tales from a Rocky Coast.
Vol. 1. Dac Says Publishing (2018)

Fiction:

Fudging (award winning)

Fantasy:

Circles
The Gemini Portal
(work in progress)

Poetry:

Ad Infinitum
The Difference
Mortal Man

Debra Davis Hinkle

Photo by Roland Hinkle

Finding Debra:
  Facebook: Debra Davis Hinkle
  Goodreads and LinkedIn

Amazon Author Page

Websites/blog:

debradavishinkle.kritiquekritics.com

fridaynightwritersgroup.com

Debra's Neonesque Artwork

Publications:

Creative Nonfiction/Fiction/poetry:

Tears to Laughter: Embracing the Future Without
Forgetting the Past
Dac Says Publishing (2012)

A Language All Their Own
Little Glimpses of the Eternal, Book 4
Short Stories
Dac Says Publishing (2017)
Page 57 - 60

Anthologies:

Tales from a Rocky Coast, Vol. 1
Dac Says Publishing (2018)
Page 57 - 111

Tales from The Corner, An Anthology
Central Coast Press (2005)
Page 139 - 143 & 209 - 212

Poetry:

Meow Poetry
Dac Says Publishing (2018)
This 'n That Poetry
Dac Says Publishing (2018)

Non-Fiction:

Almost ? Blog Post Ideas...
Dac Says Publishing (2018 - 2019)

Mom's Determination a Lifetime Gift of Devotion
The Daily Breeze
My Turn
May 9, 2017

SLO NightWriters' Newsletter
April 8, 2010, January 11, 2011

There is Another Way to Pick up Leaves
Ezine articles
November 10, 2006

Poems:

I Want My Mommy
The Tribune
April 12, 2017

Helping Hand
The Tribune
April 12, 2010

My Hand
Women's Press
July/August 2009 issue, Page 4

Shirley Radcliff Bruton

Photo by Marv Lyons

Finding Shirley:
Website:

shirleyradcliffbruton.fridaynightwritersgroup.com
Facebook: Shirley Radcliff Bruton

Shirley's performances read as poems or prose, both within her notes and spoken scripts. This work is not traditional theatre, but rather random, succinct moments seen as collages within a story. "Shirley Henderson (a.k.a. Radcliff Bruton), poet, philosopher, dancer is equally at home with visuals ...." Diana Zlotnick, *Newsletter on the Arts.*

Performances:

<u>New York</u>
Shifting Companionships, A Clear Space
Desire Caught by the Tail, an excerpt from a Pablo Picasso play, rearranged and embellished,
Merce Cunningham Dance Studio and The Kitchen
Each Move, Each Move, Each Move, Inroads
The Miller Family Foreword, Whitney Museum of American Art, Downtown
A Ceremony, Larry Richardson's Gallery

<u>California</u>
It Was Curious How They Seemed to Perform for Each Other,
Newport Harbor Art Museum and
Exploratorium, California State University Los Angeles
They Turned and Swooped and Fell Into the Force of Gravity Itself,
Los Angeles Institute of Contemporary Art
310 Prima Vera, Cats Paw Palace and
Municipal Art Gallery Theatre
Things That Move Because of Me, Union Art Gallery,
California State University Los Angeles

Some Table and Chair Decisions, Pennsylvania Avenue
Studio and Church in Ocean Park; also performed at Entopia
Theatre, Athens Greece by permission

Publications/Reviews:

Anthologies:

Tales from a Rocky Coast, Vol. 1
Dac Says Publishing (2018)

Poetry:

This 'n That Poetry
Dac Says Publishing (2018)

Atascadero Library, Discovery in Art and Poetry

Exhibition
The Tribune, Central Coast Living, From Soul to Paper
The Village Voice, Centerfold
The Soho News
The Biennial Report of *The Performance Bank*
Newsletter on the Arts, Volumes VI, VII, VIII
Los Angeles Times

Shirley lives with her husband Richard (a.k.a. Dick), two
cats, roaming deer, flying, bathing and nesting birds,
and other creatures who wander above and below
ground.

Susan Tuttle

Photo by Aaron Kondziela

Finding Susan:

Facebook: Susan Tuttle
Twitter: @STuttleWriter
LinkedIn
Goodreads

Amazon Author Page

Susan's Author Page

Website/blog:

www.SusanTuttleWrites.com

Publications:

Fiction:

Suspense Novels:	<u>Tangled Webs</u>
	<u>Piece By Piece</u>
	<u>Sins of the Past</u>
Paranormal Suspense:	<u>*Proof of Identity</u>
Historical Suspense:	<u>A Matter of Identity</u>
Short Story Collection:	<u>Death in the Valley</u>

Indie B.R.A.G. Medallion winner

Anthologies:

<u>Somewhere in Crime</u>
<u>The Best of SLO NightWriters in Tolosa Press</u>
<u>Deadlines: Murder and Mayhem on the CA Coast, Vol. 1</u>
<u>Deadlines: Murder and Mayhem on the CA Coast, Vol. 2</u>
<u>Tales from a Rocky Coast, Vol. 1</u>

Poetry:

<u>Mirror Eyes</u>

Non-Fiction:

<u>Write It Right: Exercises to Unlock the Writer in Everyone</u>
    <u>Vol. 1: Character; Setting; Story</u>
    <u>Vol. 2: Point of View (POV)</u>
    <u>Vol. 3: Plot; Dialogue</u>
    <u>Vol. 4: Scenes; Style/Voice</u>
    <u>Vol. 5: /Conflict/Tension; Subplots</u>
    <u>Vol. 6: Brilliant Beginnings; Extraordinary Endings</u>

Audio Books:

Proof of Identity
Sins of the Past

Writing as Susan Grace O'Neil

Spiritual Books:

The Journey Series:
Lord, Let Me Grow: A Journey with Jesus Through the
Parables (Volume 1)

Lord Let Me Walk: A 3-year Journey with Jesus
Through Lent

Spokescat

"Hooman, thanks for buying the book."
Ebony Renfield Hinkle